THE LEGACY SERIES

The Path of Totality
Marie Zhuikov

Shocker in Gloomtown
Dan Libman

The Continental Divide
Bob Johnson

The Three Devils and Other Stories
William Luvaas

The Correct Response
Manfred Gabriel

Welcome Back to the World: A Novella & Stories
Rob Davidson

Greyhound Cowboy and Other Stories
Ken Post

Close Call
Kim Suhr

The Waterman
Gary Schanbacher

Signs of the Imminent Apocalypse and Other Stories
Heidi Bell

What We Might Become
Sara Reish Desmond

The Silver State Stories
Michael Darcher

An Instinct for Movement
Michael Mattes

The Machine We Trust
Tim Conrad

Gridlock
Brett Biebel

Salt Folk
Ryan Habermeyer

The Commission of Inquiry
Patrick Nevins

Maximum Speed
Kevin Clouther

Reach Her in This Light
Jane Curtis

The Spirit in My Shoes
John Michael Cummings

The Effects of Urban Renewal on Mid-Century America and Other Crime Stories
Jeff Esterholm

What Makes You Think You're Supposed to Feel Better
Jody Hobbs Hesler

Fugitive Daydreams
Leah McCormack

Hoist House: A Novella & Stories
Jenny Robertson

Finding the Bones: Stories & A Novella
Nikki Kallio

Self-Defense
Corey Mertes

Where Are Your People From?
James B. De Monte

Sometimes Creek
Steve Fox

The Plagues
Joe Baumann

The Clayfields
Elise Gregory

Kind of Blue
Christopher Chambers

Evangelina Everyday
Dawn Burns

Township
Jamie Lyn Smith

Responsible Adults
Patricia Ann McNair

Great Escapes from Detroit
Joseph O'Malley

Nothing to Lose
Kim Suhr

The Appointed Hour
Susanne Davis

Janet Goldberg's compelling story collection *Like Human* brings to mind Leonard Cohen's lyric from "Anthem," "There's a crack in everything. That's how the light gets in." These are dark tales in which the stories of married couples, hiking in the natural beauty of the California wilderness, are explorations of relationships as much as of landscape, each arriving at a place where they proceed at their own peril. In the second half of the book, the narrative turns from nature to explore inner terrains, often from the viewpoint of a vulnerable young person. It is Goldberg's gift that the reader is struck again and again, not by the darkness of these compulsively readable stories but by how often even the smallest light can illuminate all.

—MJ WERTHMAN WHITE
author of *An Invitation to the Party*

Like Human is a quietly charged collection of short stories about people in motion—through deserts, mountains, suburbs, and city centers—grappling with the fragile threads that hold them together. From couples nearing their breaking point to strangers whose presence lingers too long to bears that might or might not be out to get you, each story explores the subtle ways relationships shift, unravel, or endure. With crisp prose and a steady undercurrent of unease, Goldberg captures what it means to be human and just how easily things can feel like they slip out of place.

—ROBYN DABNEY
author of *The Ascenditure*

With beautiful, evocative writing, Goldberg pulls readers into the wonders and perils of the natural world, while brilliantly capturing the complexity of the humans who roam it.

—CANDI SARY
author of *Magdalena*

A couple on the run. A marriage on the rocks. A therapist has a chance run-in with a troubled young man at a museum. On the heels of the pandemic, a widow on a hike is haunted by a rabid creature that may or may not be the devil incarnate. In *Like Human*, Janet Goldberg takes us on a delectable tour of humanity's sick souls and innocents, of nature's superb splendor and the peril therein—where one slipup can be the difference between salvation and death. In vivid prose, via stark characterizations and shocking twists, she reminds us that just as humans can leave paths of destruction, nature can engage in psychological warfare—that we are never too far from the teeming madness beneath it all.

—FREDRICK SOUKUP
author of *Blood Up North*

The stories in Janet Goldberg's *Like Human* are often set in wild places, but as the title intimates, they are centered in our most familiar territory—our relationships, always complicated, usually troubled, with partners, parents, friends, strangers. They begin and end in the middle of whatever drama is transpiring and nothing is typically resolved, but we gain from them a sympathy for her protagonists, all women, as they aspire to live free of others' constraints and expectations. With their keen eye for detail, an ear attuned to off-beat utterances, and their surreal, dreamlike settings, these stories make for lively, satisfying reading.

—RICK KEMPA
editor, *Deep Wild Journal*

LIKE HUMAN

stories

JANET GOLDBERG

CORNERSTONE PRESS

UNIVERSITY OF WISCONSIN-STEVENS POINT

Cornerstone Press, Stevens Point, Wisconsin 54481
Copyright © 2025 Janet Goldberg
www.uwsp.edu/cornerstone

Printed in the United States of America by
Point Print and Design Studio, Stevens Point, Wisconsin

Library of Congress Control Number: 2025943468
ISBN: 978-1-968148-04-1

This is a work of fiction. Names, characters, businesses, places, events, and incidents are either the products of the author's imagination or used in a fictitious manner. Any resemblance to actual persons, living or dead, or actual events is purely coincidental.

Cornerstone Press titles are produced in courses and internships offered by the Department of English at the University of Wisconsin–Stevens Point.

DIRECTOR & PUBLISHER
Dr. Ross K. Tangedal

EXECUTIVE EDITORS
Jeff Snowbarger, Freesia McKee

EDITORIAL DIRECTOR
Brett Hill

SENIOR EDITORS
Paige Biever, Eva Nielsen, Reilly Crous

PRESS STAFF
Alex Diaz, Kimberly Janesch, Ryleigh Miller, Abby Paulsen, Josh Paulson, Leo Poskozim, Sam Zajkowski, Sophie McPherson, Madison Schultz, Autumn Vine, Samantha Bjork

For Tim

Stories

Goldfish & Women 1

Every Small Thing 10

The Hike 20

Ursa Major 26

Nell 35

Desert Draw 44

Hurt 52

The Fugitive Widow 60

Safe 71

Rock, River, Salmon, Sky 82

Like Human 93

The Keeper 102

The Prank 113

A Proper Ballerina 124

A Pretty Picture 135

El Diablo 143

Little People 152

Back to Eve 161

Acknowledgments 173

Goldfish & Women

We hadn't heard from Big Ray in over a year. Big Ray had been my husband Jake's tennis buddy from the Rose Garden, and the person who'd introduced me to Jake. Not that I'd been much of a player back then—after a set of lessons, I'd kept myself to the wall, hitting the ball over the wall and chasing it like an imbecile. Center court was where the so-called good players—or jerks—played, guys who hit hard, entered and blew local tournaments, and screamed "fuck" when they missed a shot or got a bad call. Some worked jobs; others didn't. A few still lived with their mothers. In the small world of the Berkeley Rose Garden, a multi-tiered amphitheater of rose bushes, flagstone, and bay view, they'd become stars. Both Ray and Jake had played center court long before I'd made my appearance, and it was Ray who first approached me at the wall. Then, after a few dates—dinner and not much else—one day at the Rose Garden he introduced me to Jake, and after the three of us hit the ball around we went for pizza. And that's how I ended up switching—marrying Jake, at the Rose Garden of course, a cheap rent for a weekend wedding. All the guys on the courts that morning who weren't invited ceased fire at the net, racquets politely lowered as we spoke our vows, *thou shalt no longer waste endless hours playing tennis at the Rose Garden* being one of our most profound. One of the unintended results of that vow, though, was that Jake and Ray had mostly lost touch. A month after the wedding, Ray had stopped by to drop off T-shirts, gifts from a trip to China; after that, we never heard from him, and for some reason Jake never called him. But now, after a one-year silence, Ray had rung us up, giddy and in love. Did we want to meet for breakfast?

The following weekend when we pulled up to Ray's two-story duplex, one of many buildings his parents owned, we spotted Ray at the back of his driveway, standing by the garage. He was wearing his usual silky green tennis shorts, and he had his hands on his hips. His black hair, tinged with gray, was sticking up static-electricity style, and there was no sign of the woman.

"Hey, Big Ray!" Jake said, halfway up the driveway, reaching out his hand.

Ray met him halfway, Ray, short and stout, Jake, tall and lean, the bush and the tree, what the Rose Garden regulars had called them.

"Jake, buddy boy," Ray said, slapping him on the back. "Long time no see." Ray scrambled back to the garage, picked up a racquet, and swung a quick backhand. "When we going to play? Double or nothing." Ray's eyes twinkled. He put down the racquet, then looked at me. "Sarah" slid out of his mouth like a question, the *rah* rising.

"Ray," I said, peering at the toothy ramparts snaking across his T-shirt, the same Great Wall shirt he'd given Jake and me. He'd come back with a thousand of them to peddle at flea markets. Fluorescent green, the shirts were supposed to glow in the dark, but mine never made it on my body and Jake's had disintegrated in the wash. Now I could see that the other 997 shirts piled on a lawn chair in the garage corner amidst the wreckage of other failures: piles of twisted clothes, stacks of paperbacks—25 cents each—and old record albums. Naked babes, not for sale, were strewn on the floor, still glossy on the covers of dog-eared *Playboys*. Stepping into the garage, I walked over to an open carton, in it his best invention—the Ray Wang Panic Box, a rectangular gadget dotted with multicolored buttons, each emitting a noxious sound—siren, bark, horn, scream. When pushed, its purpose was to ward off the dreaded mugger or lurking rapist. The problem was, though, the buttons were so sensitive they'd go off by accident, scaring the hell out of you and everyone else. That's why I'd never used mine.

"What's all this?" Jake said, standing on the driveway near some hedges.

I stepped back onto the driveway and went over to Jake. "My god," I said, looking down at the plump iridescent bodies of goldfish, their heads shorn off. There must have been a dozen of them scattered along the far side of the driveway.

"Oh," Ray said, the smile slipping from his face, "we had a little accident here last night." He looked back at the garage. "That's why I moved the tank in there."

I looked back at the garage. Inside it, off to the left, in the corner, on the floor, was a shallow wooden crate, a bizarre, makeshift tank.

"Cats?" Jake asked.

"Raccoons," Ray said.

I put my hands on my hips. "Jack the Ripper, I'd say. Why didn't you just buy a real fish tank?" I looked at the dead fish again, their lovely, scalloped fins shriveled up and bloodied.

"A family," Ray said. "They've been getting into everyone's garbage." He shook his head. "God, this is terrible. I need to get these out of here before Ginny comes down. She's taking a shower. She's a vegetarian." Crouching down, he started collecting the bodies and chucking them in the garbage. Between fish, he glanced up at me, blinking his eyes nervously. He knew I knew something about fish—I'd raised tropical fish as a child—and gambling from my bankrupt father. That kept our dates going for a while since Ray gambled too.

Feeling sick, I walked back into the garage to the tank, which was lined with plastic. Squatting down, I peered into the water, the oxygen softly bubbling, and wondered what it would be like, fins propelling my body through the inky water, the undulating moon suddenly shattered, shredded. They likely didn't feel anything. Still, I shuddered.

Ray came into the garage and, squatting beside me, brushed his arm against mine. "Look," he said. "They didn't all die."

A fantail with silky red and white fins floated by obliviously.

Ray smiled. "She's a beauty, isn't she?"

"She is," I said, peering at the other survivors. Huddled down deep in the corners, they looked ghostly.

"Where'd you get them?" I asked.

"That trip to China. My parents sent me to find a wife."

"Doesn't this shut?" Jake asked. Behind us, he was trying to pull the garage door down.

Ray stood up and turned to a large piece of cardboard leaning against the wall. "See, I'm building a barricade, a wall."

I stood up and peered at the collage of cardboard he'd taped together. "Ray," I said, "that won't hold."

"Hey." A high-pitched voice came from above. We all stepped out of the garage. Standing at the top of the back steps was the woman, the love of Ray's life, a Caucasian mermaid, her long strings of wet hair hanging over her shoulders, staining her blouse, her right arm in a sling. Barefoot and skinny, she looked young and girlish, but as she came down the steps she seemed to age, eyes puffy, skin saggy, face a little crooked. I couldn't help but stare at a pink gash across the bridge of her nose as she slipped her good arm around Ray and smiled pleasantly. "Did Ray tell you what happened?"

WAITING FOR OUR NAMES to be called, we milled among other couples outside Sammy's, a popular diner sandwiched between the San Francisco Bay and the warehouse district. The neighborhood, a no-man's land a year ago, had gone through a renaissance, spruced up by boutiques and cafes and weekend shoppers with shopping bags. In the distance, a train was blowing its whistle mournfully. When it was out of earshot, I said, "Jake grew up near the railroad. The whistle reminds him of his childhood." I didn't know why I'd said it. I looked over at Jake, and he laughed. "Whatever you say, hon." Shrugging, he man-glanced over at Ray knowingly. I recognized that look: *What will she think of next?*

Nevertheless, I blathered on. "In the corner of our bedroom is Jake's boyhood dresser. He won't let me throw it away. He wants me to refinish it."

"Ginny," Ray said, jumping in, "wants to tear up the front yard."

Ginny rolled her eyes. "Tear up the ivy jungle, put poppies in. What a crime!"

"That would be pretty," I said, "lots of orange and green." I eyed Ray—he was smiling, loving it—in love for the moment.

A girl in a Sammy's Diner T-shirt stepped through the door, onto the sidewalk, and shouted my name. The diner, a spiffy 50s style place with black and white tile and red booths, was buzzing with chatter. We slid into the booth and cracked open the menus. Everything here was large and overpriced, but the food was good. The jukebox blasted Elvis, and even if you weren't happy when you walked in, you couldn't help swinging your leg to the beat. Beneath the table, my knee bumped time against Jake's, and he rested his hand on it, making it stop. The waitress, a cute blonde in a tight white outfit and one of those tiara-type visors on her head, pulled out her order pad and we ordered away. Then, Jake said to Ginny, "Ray told me about your fellowship at the lab. Congratulations." He was referring to Lawrence Berkeley Lab, up in the hills, among the eucalyptus groves, where no one knew exactly what they did—supposedly secret government work.

"Thanks," Ginny said, "but actually I'm still trying to get my dissertation finished."

"Ginny's on the twelve-year plan," Ray said. "Her cyclometer keeps breaking down."

Chuckling, I pronged a wedge of pancake, the word sounding funny coming out of Ray's mouth, and I wondered if Ginny knew about Ray's neat piece of physics, the male version of the Ray Wang Panic Box—a little black gun he kept in the freezer behind the Rocky Road, for protection in case he won big at Pai Gow, his favorite card game. He'd said it was a .22.

"It measures revolutions of particles, the cyclometer," Ray said, egg quivering on his fork, en route to his mouth.

"An accelerator that propels particles in spiral paths," Ginny added.

"Sarah took physics for poets in college," Jake said, placing strips of salmon on his bagel. Skinny as he was, he was getting the beginnings of a tire, so he was bulking up on fatty acids or something like that.

"Actually," I said, "I took horticulture." But I didn't know any more about plants than I did about physics or guns. I was going to say something about fish, about mollies and the kinds of diseases they get, how you should never mix them with other fish, but our waitress was at our booth. "What else can I get you?" and when no one said anything, she plunked down the check, and the topic changed, Ginny telling about her accident a few weeks ago, a fall off a bike, a broken jaw, fractured shoulder, how the paramedic had said, *Hey, what are you crying about—you're not that hurt.* That's when Ray's hand turned all snaky, tangling and untangling his fingers with hers. "That bastard," Ginny said, and Ray leaned over and kissed her on the cheek.

I tried not to but kept looking at the pink scar on her nose and out of my mouth popped, "Will you be making nuclear weapons after you get your degree?"

"Sarah!" Jake reached for my shoulder, but he caught his glass and sent it over the edge of the table to the floor where it broke with a crash, and I almost started laughing, Jake, always complaining how I manhandled everything, how once I opened a cabinet in a fancy store and the door snapped back and the ugly vase on top tumbled to the floor, shattering. The truth was, Jake was worse than me. A serial breaker, he broke a glass practically every time he did the dishes. I could never keep a set of four intact.

A WEEK AFTER our breakfast, on my way to the post office, I detoured past Ray's place. Jake was at work, and I wasn't working. Time on my hands, six months according to my obstetrician, I had just hit the first trimester mark, but I hadn't told Jake yet. After miscarrying the first one, I didn't want to jinx this one. I was in front of Ray's place now. It was still the eyesore of the neighborhood, the lovely 1920s building peeling, its veranda rusted, its face stripped of its wooden windows replaced by aluminum ones. The driveway was even messier than last week, cluttered with janitor-style garbage cans on wheels, a flying saucer-shaped hot tub, odd pieces of wood and an old lawn mower, and Ray's old two-seater car. I walked up the driveway a little and, peering around his car, saw him in the garage tearing down the cardboard wall he'd cobbled together for the surviving fish. As I made my way toward him, I said, "The best way to protect oneself and others is to construct a barrier that can't be sacked, one that will deter hostile intruders or at least hold them off for a period of time."

"What?" Ray said, turning toward me.

"It's from *Civilization and its Barriers*, Chapter Two, 'Great Wall Mythology.'" I had a photographic memory, but no one ever believed me.

"Right," Ray said, turning back to his wall. "Is that what you came to tell me? You know I've been to the Great Wall. I've walked it."

"You're lucky," I said. "You know, you ought to turn this place into a museum." Then something caught my eye, something of my own among the heaps of garage-sale junk, an old biddy black velvet dressing gown with gold tinsel sleeves I'd won in a raffle at Macy's lingerie department where I used to work. It was swirled up on a folding chair, and atop it was a sleeping albino cat, a real one. "Jesus, Ray, what happened to it?"

"That's Snowy. He's a runaway."

"I mean his ears?"

"Cancer. Ginny and I split the cost of amputation."

"That's gross." I touched my ear, then bent down and picked up a bookmark. On it was a shot of a girl in a bikini top. I waved it at him. "Hey, you never made a go of this, huh?"

Ray laughed. "No, but me and Jake sure had fun doing it."

He was referring to a time long before I'd come into the picture, before I'd ever been to the Rose Garden, when he and Jake, young and stupid, had cruised the U.C. Berkeley campus secretly snapping pictures of coeds' body parts to be put on bookmarks and laminated.

Ray stepped away from the wall and squatted down beside the tank, mulling over his fish. "They're still skittish," he said.

"They've been through a lot," I said, squatting down beside him.

"I'm putting a screen over the tank at night now. So far so good."

"Their claws are so agile. They can pick locks, unbutton dresses. They're vicious. I've seen them." I wiggled my fingers.

Ray considered my hands then grabbed a bunch of fish pellets and tossed them into the tank. "Hey," he said, "watch these guys."

We watched the pellets float; the fish, though, kept to their corners.

"They're still traumatized," I said. I looked over my shoulder. "Where's Ginny?"

Ray tossed in more pellets. "Oh, come on you guys." He pleaded with his fish.

"Oh." I pressed my hand to my stomach. I felt a twinge of something, and I thought of the bloody mess floating in the toilet, of clots of fish matter when a long time ago I'd let tank water get too warm and cooked a litter of baby angels.

"You okay?" Ray asked.

"You know it's only a matter of time before the raccoons get through the screen."

He studied the tank for another minute, then reared back on his heels and plopped down in an empty lawn chair. "Ginny left."

I stood up and walked over to the carton of panic boxes. I pulled one out, still a sleek, nifty thing, with a flashlight at the top and all its colored buttons set in a dial like a cycle of birth control pills. "You know I still have mine," I said.

"Really?" He lifted his eyes. "You carry it with you?"

"I'm pregnant," I said, then pushed a button. A siren pierced the air. The cat sprung off the chair.

"Hey, you must be happy," Ray said.

I pointed to where the cat had been. "What's that doing there?"

Ray reached over for the gun, and before I could say anything he pressed it to his temple and pulled the trigger. "Piece of junk. Never even worked." He tossed it over to the lawn chair, the 997 T-shirts breaking its fall.

Every Small Thing

L**ittle** grew up here: only the cut-leaved daisy and the evening primrose clung precariously to the sides of the trail. That's how *Sierra High Country*, my husband's trail book, described the Sonora-Pass-to-Kennedy-Meadows hike, making it sound romantic if not a bit desperate. Hiking it had been my husband's idea, though I doubt the fate of a daisy or any flower troubled him much. The larger views were his forte, and this trail offered one such view only two miles up. Still, the book rated the trail "very strenuous," warning against children and "novice hikers navigating its steep corridors" before the winter snowfields had melted. When I pointed this out to my husband as he turned the car off Route 108 into the Sonora Pass parking lot, he said, "You're not a child and it's August," and he was right, no meanness in it, though others might have read his flatness differently. Either way, I could always bail, and this time I had good reason to. I was suffering bouts of morning sickness, what my husband thought was tail-end flu. Waiting for the right moment to tell him had taken longer than I'd expected.

The car parked, we stood at the edge of the lot, 9,000 feet up, and scanned the vista, the pass, a wind-swept saddle of mountain, rock, and tree. As I'd slept in, keeping my up-at-dawn husband waiting, it was already midday—late by hiking standards—and though the sun was strong, the wind cut through me. By late afternoon, it would get stronger, gathering itself from a long distance like a wave, then break across the mountains, howling through the trees. While I put on my windbreaker, my husband stuffed the pack with food—bread, nuts, chocolate, salami. Waiting, I peered at a one-man tent pitched near a steep drop. Two horses, lassoed to a rope between trees, were bobbing their heads. A man in a cowboy hat, crouched near a campfire pit, was whittling something with a knife. I wanted to ask my husband what kind of work the man did, how he stood the high-country night, the wind battering his tent, but my husband had already slammed the trunk closed and slipped the pack straps over his shoulders. "Ready?" He handed me the water bottle. It swung from my hand like a lantern as we cut across the lot and Highway 108 and threaded our way up-slope, through trees, until we came to a wooden post. The trail sign, usually nailed to the top, had been ripped off. With my finger, I touched the small, rough hole where the nail had been and felt a sharp prick. "Ouch!"

My husband lifted my hand to inspect the tip of my finger. "Splinter," he said.

"Figures," I said, thinking the missing sign prophetic.

"You should be more careful," my husband said, reaching into the pack, while I crouched down, picked up a stick, and poked through the brush with it. Maybe it was my condition—three months in and I was already thick about the waist and pasty white—that made me queasy about my husband jabbing at me with a needle in the woods. Maybe it was because once or twice he'd mumbled something about the infirmity of the body resulting from infirmity of the mind and maybe in my mind I'd gotten it all twisted up and thought pregnancy was an infirmity of the mind. Then again, his ex had been infirm three times over. Whatever the case, I'd planned to let the news slip on the trail, but not now, not with that needle between his fingers and a splinter in mine. "Let's wait till we get back to the room," I said, trying to put an end to it.

But instead of dropping it, my husband crouched down beside me and said, "You won't feel a thing," as he ran the needle over the dark wedge of splinter, and I shuddered against that strange hybrid of pleasure and pain.

"What exactly are you hunting for anyway with that stick?" he asked.

The head of the splinter exposed, he switched to tweezers while I, with my other hand, still held the stick and kept poking at the brush. An earring, leash, pacifier, keys, a glove, a sock—people were always leaving tokens of themselves at trailheads, and I was a collector of such tokens, an amateur archeologist, as my husband liked to call me. It was a strange habit, I knew, but I'd cultivated strange habits throughout my life. As a child, I'd raided closets and dressers, going through pockets, looking for any fragment—phone numbers written on matchbooks, notes scribbled on bits of paper, old shopping lists, receipts—that hinted at something beyond an ordinary life.

"Voila!" My husband said, holding the splinter between the tweezers like a trophy. "Should we add it to your collection?" He handed me a Band-Aid. "I'm going to scoot ahead, scout out the trail. I'll be right back."

I rose to my feet. "Wait," I said, wrapping my finger, giving up the dig.

As we walked, we sank a little into the moist, fragrant earth, and I glanced over my shoulder at my boot prints, my trail of breadcrumbs, my only tether to my point of origin—the trailhead and the lot we'd parked in. Soon we emerged into the sun, and a kind of Eden opened before us. Yellow mule ears, nested in palms of pointed leaves, banked a pretty silver stream. After we crossed this stream its twin appeared, this one flocked by sprays of pinkish-purple shooting star, monkey flower, and elephanthead. I'd been studying my field guide, taking samples home, and matching them to habitats and pictures. I liked their names. Crouching down, I plucked a star and peered into its center, its "dark purple nose," as the guide called it. Meanwhile, my husband walked up ahead. Every now and then I glanced up at him to make sure he hadn't disappeared. Out here I was prone to such thoughts, but, as always, my husband's neat, agile body was in view, and I watched it with fascination the way I'd watch an animal—a deer or coyote poised pensively in the woods—until he spotted me and, laughing, said, "You can get arrested for that, you know."

"Only if you turn me in." I slipped the star into my pocket, along with the Band-Aid wrapper. He was right, though. This was, after all, a national forest. National forests had laws. Standing up, I lifted my chin toward the barren mountain of scree. "Is that it?"

My husband pointed. "See the switchbacks?"

Narrow and steep, the book had warned, the trail would zigzag up a 1,000 feet per mile through lodgepole pine, origi-nally contorted dwarf trees that flourished along the California coast. Harsh Sierra conditions, according to the book, had managed to straighten them out though, making it easier for local Indians to make teepees out of them.

"Well?" I said, still peering up at the mountain, at the switchbacks.

"It's late," he said, looking at me, "but I think we can make the first clearing, then do the rest of the trail another time. What do you think?"

My eye traveled up to the blue sky, the sun perched high in it; then I glanced back at the oasis of lovely wildflowers below, my small piece of Eden where I could nose shoot-ing stars with impunity, then back over to the mountain of pumice—the type of rock women used to slough off dead skin—and planted my foot on the trail, feigning enthusi-asm. Stepping in front of my husband, I gingerly mounted the first switchback and continued up at a quick clip, my heart beating double time in the thin air. I always started quick, as if a trail were something to get over with rather than savor, hiking more my husband's passion than mine. After taking three more switchbacks, I stopped to let my husband catch up with me. I was starting to sweat, so I took off my jacket and tied it around my waist. I took a couple of deep breaths. At this altitude, it always took me a while to straighten out my heart, to breathe comfortably. As my husband approached, I turned back around and continued up. With each switchback taking us up to a higher shelf of mountain, the trail became more and more exposed, so I kept my eye to the inside bank, the gray face of the mountain. Then I heard the crunch and slide of rock. Now people were coming toward us. People up here were a relief. At sea level, my husband and I did without them; we'd cultivated few friendships since we'd married and let those we had drift. The mailman was the only person we saw on a regular basis.

Hi. Hello. Hey. The two men and woman each greeted us as we pressed our backs to the face so they could pass. As I watched the trio descend—the woman, last in line— shrinking away from us, I said, "Do you think any of them will remember us?"

"What do you mean?"

"If we got lost or killed."

Sighing, my husband turned away from me taking in the view—dense treetops obscuring the twin streams and beyond a slice of 108 and its double yellow line. Then he looked at me, as if he'd just heard me. "Your lips are cracked," he said. "You'd better drink. Drink more than you think."

"Very witty," I said, unscrewing the cap and taking a sip while my husband stepped in front of me and took the lead. I lagged up behind him, my mind still working the idea of us disappearing: *Oh yeah, I saw her. She was with a man, tall and wiry, with a frayed orange backpack, beige shorts, and a green jacket. Older than her. Hers was red with a hood, and she was wearing a ponytail.*

Catching up with my husband, I said, "We should have asked."

My husband took the water from me, and he, of the beige shorts and frayed backpack, drank.

I looked up at the sky. Clouds were coming in, and the wind had gotten gustier. I slipped my jacket back on and pressed my feet together. Parallel, they were a snug fit across the narrow trail. Worse yet, the trail had gone from flat to sloped, so the right side of my body was tilted lower than my left, throwing me off center. One misstep with nothing but slippery scree to grab onto and I'd end up, if I were lucky, in the wild-flowered stream where I could bathe my cut-up flesh. Such half-pleasant thoughts fueled me up several more switchbacks until we reached a plateau, a small stand of lodgepoles. Huddled together, they looked like tall, skinny Christmas trees that hadn't filled in. Their spiky, ornament-shaped cones were scattered on the ground among a carpet of needles. "Good shelter during a storm," I said, wrapping my arms around my waist. "Weather's getting worse. Maybe we should abort."

"Right up there," my husband said, pointing, "is a clearing, where the view is. The edge of the world, the book said."

The wind lashed my hair into my eyes. I touched the back of my head. Somewhere along the trail I'd lost my hair band.

My husband lifted my hood and tied the string under my chin. "You don't have to look, and we can eat a quick lunch, then head back down. The weather will hold." He kissed me on the cheek, then started up again, and I followed, crouched over, trying to get under the wind. Ten minutes later the clearing, a barren, rocky landscape, came into view, and in the lull between gusts we heard voices. Clusters of people were crouched down, some behind boulders, others in small craters, sheltering themselves.

"Here," my husband said, pulling me behind a vacant boulder. Squatting, he opened the backpack and took out a paper plate. Lifting his hand off it, it sailed through the air and over the edge. I was tempted to rise to my feet, follow its trajectory, but I was queasy. Whether it was altitude, hunger, or morning sickness I didn't know.

"We'll use the pack," my husband said, flattening it to the ground like a tablecloth. On it he laid chunks of salami, chocolate, and bread. As he ate, tearing salami with his teeth, ants erupted from the ground. A chipmunk appeared and twitched its nose. My husband tossed it an almond, and it gnawed greedily at it. Meanwhile, I popped my head around the boulder and eyed the strange plateau and the groups huddled down on it. They could have been tribes of a pre-historic planet or survivors on a post-nuclear planet. *Little grew up here.* The sentence from the book echoed in my mind, and it was hard to believe that we'd just come from a place of lushness, the twin streams, and all that nourished it. Shivering, I retreated back behind the boulder while my husband replaced me at the helm.

"Look," he said.

A man and a woman passed us, continuing along the trail. Clad in slickers and tightly hooded, they carried enormous packs and leaned on walking sticks. Where they were going I couldn't say. To follow the rest of the trail required a steep descent down a short hill that would have easily toppled me, sans backpack. At the brink of it, the couple paused, then starting down, disappeared out of view. Then they reappeared at the bottom and began crossing a flat area, a hard-crusted desert of sorts, heading toward a strange remnant of cave, a craggy mouth, a stone ring, at the edge of the earth. Step off it and you'd drop off, I imagined, and as I watched the couple shrink toward it and step through it one by one, dis-appearing from my sight, it seemed as if they *had* dropped off. My husband, retreating back behind the boulder, started packing up the food, and I helped, hoping he planned to head back down. But once he slipped the straps on his shoulders and stood, he said, "Let's go a little farther. Check it out."

"You're kidding," I said. "If it rains, we're dead. The footing…" I said, knowing it was of no use. At sea level he hated rain. Rain melted the Wicked Witch of the West. Up here, though, he was oblivious.

As we headed toward the steep hill, I paused and looked back. The groups that had been hunkered down were now rising, slouching back down the trail. I could easily turn, I knew, and become one of them, and no one, except my husband, would care. But I was already at his heels following, my body unable to catch up with my thoughts. At the brink of the hill, we, like the couple before us, peered down its incline. It was smooth and speckled with rock. The ground was so hard it held no footprints.

"I'd have to go down on my rear," I said, thinking even if I made it, teetering on the edge of a big view would make me queasy all over again. The only macro-view I'd ever enjoyed was the Grand Canyon. Even in its vastness it seemed touch-able. Everything else was postcard. "Why don't you go?" I finally said, knowing it was, as always, up to me if I wanted to follow. "I'll wait." I shuddered, suppressing my twinge of fear, blaming it on the cold. What if he didn't come back? What if he stepped through that ring of stone, like the couple, and disappeared? Separating on the trail was never a good idea. I looked up at the sky. Drops were coming down. I pressed my palms to my abdomen. Something in there was stirring.

"I'll be five minutes," my husband said. "Don't worry."

"Right. Fifteen is more like it," I said, eyeing the landscape, the distance between two points, thinking how my husband had in the past overestimated himself, how he'd disappeared on me before, once on a steep trail like this in Zion National Park, so narrow and exposed that it was chained. On that, I'd inched my way along the cliff awkwardly, clasping the chain hand over hand, until the trail suddenly protruded out in a rounded arc, a kind of apron, that hung exposed, a thousand feet up. The footing, the rock itself, was both cratered and smooth, slick like rock polished by current. For me, the trail had ended there.

Back behind the boulder now, I watched my husband's progress across the flats. The rain held, but the wind still gusted, and I shivered against it, thinking how easily a body—concoction of water, salt and bone—could be blown about, how nine months could mix it all up.

My husband, at the stone ring now, looked dwarfed, infant-like, a miniature of a man. Maybe he was pondering his view and once he had his fill he'd turn back and we'd head down, and when we got to the twin streams, I'd let the news slip. But he was still there, foot perched on the ring, palm against it, trying to decide whether or not to walk through it, probably thinking how what was behind kept him behind. That's how leaving began, I thought, huddling back behind the rock, curling up against it. I looked at my watch. Eight more minutes. The truth was in Zion the trail *hadn't* ended at the chained apron for me. After ten minutes, I'd convinced myself my husband wasn't coming back. I had no good reason to think so, but still the thought had gnawed at me until I gave in and mounted the apron. Grabbing for the chain, hand-over-hand, I'd edged myself around part of the arc, until I reached its outermost point. Fully exposed, I froze, my knuckles white, until another hiker came around the bend and pried my hands off, helping me edge my way back. A few minutes later, my husband returned.

The rain was coming steady now, and I could feel it touch my cheeks and nose, taste it in my mouth. I looked at my watch again. Five more minutes. I shook my head, fighting myself, fighting the magnification of every small thing the wilderness imposes on you as I watched the last group slouch onto the trail, watched them recede from me just as the ant and the chipmunk had, one to his tunnel, the other to his hole—everything to its place. Where was mine? Was it here waiting for my husband, waiting for what was inside me to grow, or was it with the last group out, tailing them down? I got up to my knees and peered out behind the rock again, but I could hardly see the stone ring through the rain. The clouds had descended and wrapped the flats in a gauzy vapor. If my husband was out there heading back, I couldn't see him or he me, so I called out, "Hey! Hey! Anybody there?" Then I sat back behind the rock. My jacket was soaked through, my feet wet. I pulled my knees up to my chest, then felt in my pocket for the Band-Aid wrapper and the flower, the shooting star I'd plucked from below. Pulling that out, I touched its face, which was already dying, its stem wilting, cut off from the earth. I glanced at my watch. One more minute. I thought of the stands of lodgepole pines that the Indians carved into shelters, and I thought of the man in the cowboy hat and the lassoed horses. What had he been whittling with his knife? I thought of everything that came before me as I let the flower drop and then the Band-Aid wrapper. It tumbled along the wet earth, waxy paper, the thin red string that split it neatly open still attached. Maybe someone would find it.

The Hike

While my husband drove, I read a description of the Mt. Rose Trail from the brochure we'd picked up at the Lake Tahoe Chamber of Commerce. "The trail," I told my husband, quoting from the brochure, "is strenuous, twelve miles round trip, and sparsely populated." Because we would have a three-hour drive back home after the hike, I suggested we hike the Hidden Beach to Twin Lakes Trail instead—only two-and-a-half miles each way.

But my husband, a veteran of Yellowstone and Yosemite, insisted. He pulled the car off the road and took the brochure out of my hands. He read aloud, quoting from it, "Unbridled views of dormant volcanoes and glaciated canyons await you." Knowing I had bad knees, he assured me that the Mt. Rose hike would be gradual.

My husband turned the car onto Highway 431 and stopped behind a construction truck with a revolving light. While we waited for it to lead us down the resurfaced road, a long line of cars soon formed behind us.

When we finally moved, I watched the truck's huge tires crush and spit pebbles. After fifteen minutes, the pebble road turned into pavement, and the truck made a U-turn, leaving us on our own. Near the summit, we turned off onto the shoulder and let the cars behind us pass.

According to the map, the trailhead was nearby. My husband got out of the car and opened the trunk. I followed, watching cars speed by us—young couples, I imagined, on their way to Reno to marry or gamble. As I tried to fold the map into a neat triangle, I wondered how many of them would make it and how much they would lose.

My husband unzipped his orange knapsack and packed it with hard salami, French bread, plums, and paper toweling. In the pockets, he put a first-aid kit, a knife, and a tube of sunscreen. He slipped the knapsack on his back and handed me a canteen of ice. We crossed the street and walked up to a sandy hill to two wooden posts. "Mt. Rose Trail" was carved into the face of one. On top of the other I saw a silver earring. I picked it up, lifted it to the sun, and wondered if anyone would ever come back for it.

As we began the first mile, insects rose up from the ground in front of our feet. Their wasp-shaped bodies were the color of the path, dust-brown, making it difficult for us to avoid them. Unlike wasps, these insects didn't sting but buzzed away in annoyance.

The sun was hot, unusually hot, at this altitude. I expected a cool breeze, just enough to refresh me when I felt fatigued. After the third mile, I discovered the only relief was the occasional shade of a tree and a gulp from the canteen. I offered my husband a drink. He shook his head *no*. Taking my husband's baseball cap off my head, I wiped my forehead. Then I glanced over at him. He wore my wide-brimmed burgundy hat. Laughing, I told him he looked like a pimp, a drug dealer, someone not to be trusted. Pretending to be the villain, he smirked, pulled on the ends of his gray-tipped mustache and narrowed his eyes.

When the trail became steeper, I often looked out in front of me to see when it would level out again. Ahead, I saw a dog, a golden retriever, wet and dripping, running toward us, his mouth hanging open in a smile. The dog ran past us, and a young couple followed on mountain bikes at a dangerous speed over rocks and branches. We all exchanged quick nods. A few minutes later, I looked back, even though I knew they'd no longer be there.

We stopped for lunch at a small grouping of trees. A hundred feet beyond, there was a pond. After we finished lunch, we walked down to the pond and found a leash we guessed the two bikers must have left. My husband put it in the knapsack and said, "Remind me to leave this at the trailhead." Then, after walking around the pond looking at its tiny black fish, we cut across the field and picked up the trail.

From there, the trail moved gradually uphill and began curving. There were no more flat stretches. Often, I had to stop to drink from the canteen. The back of my husband's T-shirt was damp from sweat, yet he hardly drank at all.

After an hour, we came to a utility station with a pickup parked in front. I was relieved to find something motorized this high up. My husband walked past the station, looking for the trail, but the trail seemed to end there. We saw the dusty peak of Mt. Rose next door to us but found no trail that led there, so we continued along a ridge that led to a clearing, where I noticed small piles of dung, some fresh, some dried. Two deer, male and female, lifted their delicate chins and glanced at me but ran off before I could point them out to my husband.

We finally came to the edge of a cliff. "We must have missed a turn," my husband said.

"I think you mean we hiked up the wrong mountain."

He walked away from me, then turned, and said, "When we cut across the field, we missed a turn. See?" He pointed.

I looked down at the pond and, alongside it, at the fork we'd missed. "I think we should go back. I don't see any way we can get to Mt. Rose from here." I sat down and rested my burning feet. Blisters were forming on my toes.

"I think we can get back quicker if we hike straight down." My husband shielded his eyes from the sun with his hand. He turned to me, and I looked up into his face, into the lines circling the edges of his mouth and his eyes. I thought about the centers of trees, how the circles of rings measure their lives.

My husband put his sunglasses back on. He didn't seem disappointed. He dealt with this problem the way he'd deal with a mathematical problem—find a logical solution.

"Maybe we should go back where we came from." I tried to find a fault in his logic. "We already got lost once."

"But this would be a lot shorter. We can pick up the trail down there." He pointed again.

I looked. He was right, I thought, but still I had a bad feeling. I thought about the deer I'd seen earlier, their slender legs carrying them up the steep slope. Last summer a deer had come down from the Berkeley Hills to the Rose Gardens where we live. Some man in a pickup hit the deer and sent her body reeling. Right in the middle of the street, he got out of his truck and nonchalantly stabbed the deer in the heart with a switchblade. A woman tried to stop him, but he pushed her away and left the deer on the side of the street against the curb.

"Okay," I sighed, "as long as it isn't steep."

We began hiking down a grassy hill side by side, stepping occasionally over rocks. As we continued downward, I noticed the grass getting thinner and the number of rocks increasing. I stopped at a steep rock quarry. "I'm not going down there. I told you I didn't want to go down any steep hills." I put one hand on my hip, knowing I sounded like a child.

My husband reached over and took the canteen out of my hand. "We're almost there." He pointed. "This doesn't look too long." He gazed down to the bottom of the quarry and began moving down. Shaking my head, I followed, trying to place my feet in the places my husband's feet left. I bent over and used my hands for balance, but rocks slipped beneath my feet, and I slid and fell. My husband, a few feet ahead, stopped and turned around. "Are you okay?"

I stood up and wiped my hands on my shorts. I moved a few more feet forward and slid again, scraping the backs of my calves on rocks. Tiny bubbles of blood formed along the scrapes. My husband stopped again, looked at me, but said nothing.

He was analyzing the situation, I thought, trying to figure out the best way to respond. Or maybe he was even thinking of leaving me there.

"Just go," I said.

We continued down. Grabbing onto rocks with my hands, I slid recklessly but didn't fall. Occasionally, I paused and watched the orange knapsack bobbing up and down on my husband's back. Looking beyond him, I hoped to see an end to this, yet all I saw was a thick grouping of trees. They looked close, but I knew they were far away.

Still bent, I continued my crawl downward. My husband was even farther ahead than before. I placed my hand on a large rock that looked sturdy, but it shifted and rolled onto my foot. I cried out and hopped up and down. I felt my tears well up, and when I saw my husband turning, I gagged a bit, trying to stifle myself. He stayed where he was, determined, I thought, not to help me. "Are you okay?" he shouted. I didn't answer. I wiped my cheeks and moved. I felt no pain in my feet, just numbness.

An hour or so later, we finally reached the trees. My husband sat down and drank from the canteen. I stayed on my feet.

He shook his head, then looked up at me. "What an ordeal. Sit down and rest." When I didn't move, he knelt in front of me, unlaced my boots and slipped them off my feet. One side of my sock was stained with blood. He ripped a few sheets of paper toweling off the roll and placed them beneath my feet. Then he pulled off my sock and cleaned my foot with antiseptic. I made it difficult for him, though, standing the whole time while he wrapped Band-Aids around my toes, pulled burrs out of my socks. He looked up at me every so often but said nothing, and I said nothing, knowing we had another three miles back. My husband offered me the canteen, and I took it and drank, thinking about the tiny black fish clustering on the shallow banks of the stagnant pond, desperate for oxygen. It was then that I decided not to remind my husband to leave the leash on the post with the earring—no one would come back for it anyway.

Ursa Major

"The bears will be coming tonight," the gray-haired man, our campground host, said as he unloaded a bundle of firewood from his truck bed. His wife, tucked in the passenger seat, peered at us curiously as if we were some new breed of camper.

"Even with the dogs?" I said, while my husband paid him for the wood. I pointed to our neighbors, a horde of young people, campers, and Jeeps. Earlier, when we'd first arrived, their three Rottweilers, mean-faced, black dogs with tan markings, had barreled toward us and then veered off, trotting back to their campsite displaying their tails docked, black bulbs.

"They come every night," the man said, absentmindedly, as he pulled a roll of money from his pants pockets and handed my husband his change.

Now tied to trees, the dogs milled, occasionally lifting their heads to glance at us. Maybe someone had complained, someone concerned about the many children playing ball, riding bikes, and foraging beneath trees to gather kindling.

Before getting in his truck, the man turned and smiled at us, "But don't worry. They won't bother you if you don't bother them."

His wife, leaning over the driver's seat, squinted at us in the early evening sun, smiled too, as if to confirm her husband's advice.

That's what people always say about wild animals, I thought, as I watched the truck pull into the next campground where a boy and girl scurried in and out of a camper with plastic containers, plates, and paper towels while their father dumped coals into the barbecue, and their mother laid a checkered cloth on the table. At least they'd be sleeping indoors tonight. I wondered if I hadn't made a mistake earlier as we'd driven up Route 108 through the woods to the campground, lying to my husband about giving camping a try.

But worried that I wouldn't like it, he'd changed our plans, had insisted that we, despite my protests, stop at the Christmas Tree Inn, a two-story motel, decorated with blinking Christmas lights, that boasted a blue pool, a sheltered hot tub, and a few fake deer perched on a grassy slope.

Pulling up in front of the lobby, my husband said, "Why don't you see if they have any rooms?"

"Really, I want to camp," I said, trying to feign enthusiasm. I got out and walked through the door to the counter.

When I got back in the car, I said, "Booked," even though they had a cancellation, and the owner had said, "Lucky you. It's hard to get a decent room anywhere around here on such short notice."

"You won't like it," my husband said, flatly.

"How would you know what I like?" I snapped, upset by my own lie. Still, I wasn't going to admit that he was probably right. We'd been at each other lately, and it was hard to stand down.

"We'll find another one." Determined to please me or himself, my husband pulled back onto the road, stopping at several motels for the next two hours, but all were full for the weekend.

My husband walked back to the tent now and began hammering stakes into the earth. I walked over to him, my hands on my hips. "Well, what do you think that campground manager meant by that?"

Knowing this was my first time camping, he said nothing, but his silence only made me press. I was a day hiker, the kind who liked to rough it for a couple of hours and be rewarded with a hot shower, a change of underwear, and a mattress. He, on the other hand, had backpacked in Lassen, Yellowstone, climbed the nearly flat face of Yosemite's Half Dome, and slept tent-free beneath the stars at ten thousand feet and let black bears walk over his body without losing a wink of sleep—or so he claimed.

Over the past five years, though, since we married, he hadn't gone up to the mountains. His old friends from college, who either married or moved, had stopped calling. Sometimes he threatened to go by himself, yet he never went. He said he didn't want to leave me alone.

My husband glanced up at me. "Look," he said, hammer poised above a stake, "there's bears in every campground. It's no big deal. Why don't you start unloading the car? You'll feel better if you do something."

"And those garbage cans," I said, pointing to the aluminum cans with lift-off lids that sat near the road. These weren't the bear-proof cans usually found in national parks but the kind people kept behind their houses in suburbia—that much even I knew.

My husband ran his fingers through his hair. He stood up and slid the poles through the loops attached to the top of the tent. "I don't know. It might be noisy tonight," he said, hesitantly, briefly abandoning his mountain-man bravado. "We could go home if you want," he said, turning to face me. "Is that what you want?"

"I don't know. Maybe." I shook my head. "No, we should stay." But I kept thinking about that story I'd read in a newspaper—how a bear had ripped a hole in a tent and dragged a woman out while she was still zipped in her sleeping bag.

Disconcerted, I walked to the car, opened the trunk, took out the cooler, the lantern, a bag of plates and utensils. Then I sat on top of the picnic table, not knowing what else to do. My own helplessness made me uncomfortable.

Our small, triangular, rust-orange tent looked primitive compared to the sturdy, high-ceilinged tents pitched at other sites—but I didn't complain, even though as a child on family vacations I'd slept in Holiday Inns with paintings of oceans on the wall, a Bible in the dresser drawer, and room service for breakfast.

My husband stepped back from the tent, brushed his hands on his pants. "Let's give it a try."

On my hands and knees, I crawled in, careful not to knock down the pole in front of the entrance. My husband came in after me. Lying on his back, he folded his hands under his head and let out a sigh.

I sniffed. "Smells like vomit." Once, when I'd worn one of my husband's old windbreakers, I'd noticed the same smell.

"Anything stored away for five years is going to stink a little." He turned his head toward me. "Anyway, it should air out by bedtime."

I crawled out into the light, dreading the night. According to that newspaper story, the rangers had found the woman covered in leaves at the bottom of a steep embankment. Part of her stomach had been eaten by the bear, and one of her ribs, torn from her chest, looked like a fossil.

Now, the faint orange hues of sunlight between the tree-top—alpenglow—offered little comfort. Soon that light too would disappear.

My husband suggested that we start dinner. He dumped coals into the pit, squirted lighter fluid over them, and tossed in a lit match, but only a few hesitant flames sprung up then sputtered out into a puff of smoke. So he squirted more fluid and kept tossing lit matches into the pit until the coals caught.

As I collected dry sticks and pinecones for the wood fire we would build at nightfall, I looked over at our neighbors and their dogs. They were gathered around their fire drinking beer and laughing. Their dogs were now lassoed to a rope strung between two trees. Running both away from and into each other, they seemed confused and excited. When I stepped closer, though, one dog abruptly stopped and glared at me, straining to the end of his noose. The other dogs, reacting, did the same. Ears pricked, they watched me as I slowly retreated to the picnic table.

My back to the dogs now, I saw other fires, orange and yellow triangles wavering in the air, marking the surrounding sites. My husband, still squatting in front of our fire, turned toward me. "Why don't you get the food? I think it's hot enough now."

I opened the cooler, unwrapped two chicken breasts, then laid them on the grate and seasoned them with salt and pepper, parsley, and paprika. Kneeling in front of the fire, I listened to the skin sizzle and warmed my hands.

My husband pumped the lantern then stuck a lit match in the opening, but the mantles, two small gauze sacks, wouldn't catch. He fooled with the thing for another fifteen minutes. "The kerosene must have evaporated," he said, baffled.

"Evaporated?" I shook my head. "You mean you forgot to fill it before we left."

"I filled it last week." He rubbed the dark stubble on his chin and cheek.

I turned the chicken over, seasoned it again, cut deep into the meat, and used the flashlight to check the bone for blood.

Later, with our car lights shining on our site, we ate hungrily. My husband always said food tasted better at altitude. This much seemed true, though I was too morose to give him credit. Instead, I gazed at him. In the strange fluorescence of the car light, he could have been anybody.

After dinner my husband suggested a moonlight walk since it was too early to sleep. Feeling better, I agreed and slipped on my down jacket, though I suspected all we would see were the distant flames and the glow of lanterns from other camps. In front of me was only darkness, and above the silhouettes of pines stirring moodily.

"The moon will light our way," my husband said. He put his arm around my shoulders. In a baritone voice, he said, "I'll protect you, my dearie."

I looked up at the moon, just a sliver, the sharp-edged stars, the gauzy Milky Way planted in the sky, and then grabbed the flashlight. As we walked, arm in arm, my husband occasionally stopped to describe a constellation. "There's the Big Dipper." He pointed out seven bright stars and several duller ones that formed the body of an animal. "Ursa Major," my husband said. "Big Bear, but the Indians thought it looked like a sick man on a stretcher."

I continued to look up. Without my husband's guidance, the stars seemed random.

When we got back to our camp, my husband poured water over the white coals. They hissed, and steam wafted into the night air. I shined the flashlight on the campground next door. The dogs, still lassoed, slept curled on the ground. Their keepers either slept in small campers or roughed it in a large bubble-shaped tent. My husband had told me that people turned in early, woke at dawn to hike. Yet I could hear voices—children singing in rounds: *Row, row, row your boat, gently down the stream, merrily merrily, merrily, merrily life is but a dream.* Our campground host had told us that church groups held summer camps for children on the other side of the river.

Tired, we decided to save our wood for the next night's fire. We crawled into the tent, wiggled feet first into our sleeping bags, trying not to knock the fragile tent over. We kept all our clothes on but our sneakers, which we placed outside. I set the flashlight between us; its circular beam illuminated the orange walls.

"This is like sleeping in a coffin," I said, as I looked at the sagging walls that threatened to cave in. Now I understood why the woman was pulled out of the tent in her sleeping bag. It would be impossible to escape a sleeping bag and a tent in the dark with a five-hundred-pound beast roaring over you. Worried, I sat up.

My husband sighed. "Turn your bag around so your head faces the entrance." But I couldn't figure out how to do that without pushing in the flimsy walls, so my husband unzipped his bag and helped me turn mine around.

Though it was fairly warm in my sleeping bag, I shivered. At the same time, I found it difficult to breathe the tent's stuffy air. I turned over on my stomach, propped myself up on my elbows, and looked out. If I tilted my head up, I could see a swatch of Milky Way.

"Turn off that flashlight, will you," my husband said. He turned over as if to sleep. He wanted to get in a full day of hiking tomorrow. Earlier, he'd marked in a hiking book the steep trails he would do alone on a solo trip another time and the moderate ones we'd do together this trip in the gently sloped Emigrant Wilderness. A daydreamer, I liked to amble along flat trails through grassy meadows dotted with wildflowers and hidden streams, while he preferred short, steep scrambles to peaks with sweeping views of dormant volcanoes.

I tried to sleep too, dozed for an hour or so, then woke, looked up at the sky, turned over, and tried to sleep again. Then I heard something—like someone in the distance pounding metal with a hammer. My husband opened his eyes. I switched on the flashlight and listened. "What's that?" I whispered.

He shielded his eyes with his hand. "Turn that off. You're going to waste the battery."

We both listened, heard nothing for a few minutes, then more pounding and a thrashing sound.

"It's the same pattern," I whispered, as I looked out the tent, shined the flashlight on the car, then toward the road, and across to the site next door but saw nothing.

My husband put in his earplugs then turned over again. I lay on my back and listened as the pounding and thrashing became louder. I shook my husband's shoulder. "They're getting closer." A garbage can tipped over, and the dogs started barking. A man yelled, "Shut up," and after a few whimpers the dogs settled down.

I looked at my husband. His eyes seemed large, unblinking. "Do you want to get in the car?" he asked.

I sat up. "Do you?"

"It's no big deal to me. I'm only awake because you're awake." He put his hands behind his head as if he were sunning himself at the beach.

"Like hell you are." I shined the light in his eyes, then out the tent, so I could measure the distance to the car.

Then there was a loud bang as a nearby can hit the ground; the dogs barked furiously, and, before we could unzip our bags, we heard a deep-bellied roar. Struggling to get out, I hit the pole with my arm, and the tent collapsed. "Oh, god," I said, as I tried to wiggle out of my bag and push the tent off my face. A foul smell made me swoon, and I felt my arm being yanked. Something was lifting me from the tent. "This way," my husband said, pulling me toward the car. Unable to see, I stumbled into the fire pit and fell to my knees. My husband pulled me up again. "This way," he said. He switched on the flashlight, led me to the car, and opened my door. Then he ran around to his side.

"Where are we going?" I asked, touching my knees.

"Are you bleeding?" He looked down at my knees, then started the car, and backed out. As we drove through the campground, we saw cans lying on their sides, garbage strewn on the ground.

"What about our stuff?" I looked out the back window.

"We'll get it after daybreak."

We turned onto a dark unpaved road, headlight illuminating a sign: *Iceberg Wilderness*. According to the trail book, it was a place most hikers avoided, full of crumbling lava peaks and barren canyons. We drove down the road anyway, taking our time, since it would be a while before the sky lightened.

At the end of the road, we stopped. My husband turned off the engine and slid down in his seat. "Try to sleep," he said, closing his eyes.

I looked out the windshield. I thought I saw shapes slowly moving in the distance, so I shut my eyes, not wanting to see anymore.

At dawn my husband woke me. "Let's hike," he said, getting out of the car.

Sitting up, I saw horses grazing on a grassy meadow. Men wearing cowboy hats carried pails to the horses.

I got out of the car, stretched my arms over my head, then walked over to my husband. Sitting on the hood, he studied the trail book. "This is the one I wanted to hike." He pointed to the page. "I can't believe we ended up here."

I rubbed my eyes. My head hurt, pounded like a hangover. My legs felt sluggish, too, my feet five sizes larger.

"Here." My husband handed me the water bottle and a bag of trail mix. "You'll feel better."

Drinking and eating, I watched a man with a bridle come up behind a horse as she dipped her nose into a pail. "Is it steep?" I asked, shivering.

"Not very. Anyway, we'll just do part of it." He put the book back in the car, grabbed the knapsack, then slipped his arm around me, leading me to the trail.

Nell

"Every year someone is killed…" My husband read the park service sign aloud. On it was a sketch of a man tumbling down a waterfall. Having seen it before, I shifted my eyes back to the real thing: Yosemite Falls unloading—crashing into a rocky pit, dissolving into foam, swirling off into the dark green Merced, and everyone trying to get a picture of it. Then, I spotted two small figures, children on all fours, climbing the wet rocks alongside the pit. Shaking my head, I glanced over at my husband, thinking how easily people die, and said, "Remember what happened to me? In the hills with the cow?"

My husband slipped his arm around my waist and said, "I remember everything you tell me." Guiding me around the clots of people to the small, wooden bridge, he narrowed his eyes into two slits and whispered in my ear, "Now, my dearie, I have you all to myself."

"Dearie," I said, peeking over my shoulder, taking one last look at the falls, "you always have me all to yourself. But what about my cow?"

He straightened up. "Okay. Which one?"

"The one that charged me, with the calf, all curled up on the grassy slope."

As we stepped off the bridge and onto the trail, my husband said, "You got too close, but I wouldn't call that charging. Who ever heard of a cow charging?" He took off his hat, a suede cowboy-style thing he'd bought on the way up. "All I remember was her galloping toward her calf and that look on your face, when you thought she was heading for you." He let out a chuckle, then put his hat back on.

Catching the side of his face, the salt-and-pepper stubble dotting his ruddy cheek, I said, "You'd better shave that thing when we get back to the lodge. You're starting to look shifty, like that cartoon character—what's his name—that kidnaps women and ties them to railroad tracks."

"Snidely Whiplash, but there's only one woman, Nell, and she always gets saved."

As I conjured up the villain, the slit of his mouth, the spindly black mustache, my husband stopped short and pointed his finger down the trail like the snout of a gun. "Look," he said.

A large, rectangular black-and-yellow metal sign was mounted on a stake between two boulders. *A Mountain Lion Has Been Sighted in This Area.* Beneath the warning, a lion was pictured. Perched on a tree limb, it lurked above two unsuspecting hikers. I peered down the trail. Flat and wide, framed by thick forest on the left and a line of trees fronting a short steep slope on the right, the trail was just as I remembered it. A quick scramble down to the right and we'd be back to civilization, Yosemite Village, within a few minutes. But farther ahead, I knew, the trail snaked inward, deeper into the forest.

Standing in front of the sign now, I took in the shape of the animal—its wide paws, triangular face, muscular flank, and long, thick tail. "Now what?" I said.

He glanced at me, then back at the sign. "Carry a big stick, and don't crouch down."

I snatched a twig off the ground. "Like this?"

He looked at the twig, then at me, as if he'd forgotten who I was and then remembered. "Sure, if you're planning to fend off a chipmunk."

I peered up at the tree above me, at the sprawl of branches, at the trunk shooting skyward. "Maybe we should have huffed and puffed up Vernal instead." Vernal was a set of falls, a tourist-strewn trail, up a steep staircase cut from cliff.

My husband, speaking to the sign, said, "There's two of us and one of him, and what's the likelihood of seeing a lion on a sunny Saturday in summer? Plus, we always do Vernal our second day in the park."

Nodding, I took my husband's hand, let him take me down the trail, knowing he was right—lions were reclusive— and wrong because in the past we'd stumbled into grizzlies feeding on berries, had been forced off a trail by a snorting bull, and chased down another by a cloud of bees. *Lucky to be alive*, I could have said aloud, but instead I let go of my husband's hand, slipped a few steps behind, and tried to focus on what was before me, the trees and the massive chunks of granite between them, but my eyes kept reverting back to the ground, to the prints in the dirt—animal or human.

My husband stopped and waited for me to catch up. "What?"

"Nothing," I said.

Eyeing me, he unscrewed the top of the water bottle. Dropping his head back, he drank.

Standing there, I watched his Adam's apple slide up and down, knowing he was thinking that nothing is always something.

"Here," he said, handing me the bottle.

I shook my head.

"You're not going to do another Grand Canyon, are you?"

He was referring to the time I'd gotten stuck at the bottom and couldn't move my legs because, according to him, I'd ignored the signs and hadn't drunk enough water.

Changing the subject, I said, "Horses—I can smell them. We're near the village, aren't we?"

"Why—you want to cut down, get something to eat?" He screwed the cap back on and then peered down the trail.

"Do you?" Looking for a sign, I moved my eyes from his face to his hands, but even his hands, nails bitten down to the cuticles, were at ease for a change, dangling at his sides. I started walking again, even though getting off trail was exactly what I wanted. But I'd already forced my husband back once before, last summer, on a trail, a beauty in British Columbia, in Banff, that started off well enough along an old set of railroad ties blooming with wildflowers, then narrowed into a single lane, slicing through hip-high willows, downslope toward a lake. What had spooked me was a woman coming from the opposite direction. Passing us, she'd turned away, but I still caught a glimpse of her face—bitter and unhappy. And there'd been a warning at the trailhead, just a lone sentence from the Park Service about a sow and her cubs spotted on the trail, no sketch of a menacing grizzly as there had been on the signs in Montana's Glacier National Park, where we'd been a few days before. There, I'd tied bells to my shoelaces, jangling my way through the wilderness.

Now, though, there was no woman, no one at all on the trail but us, and the endpoint this time wasn't a lake six miles deep into the Canadian wilderness but the Ahwahnee, only a few miles away, a swanky granite and timber hotel named after Indians that had gathered food in the valley by day and left at dusk, afraid of spirits that dwelled among the dark cliffs.

As we continued walking, the trail curved back out, and I saw the familiar gray barn of the Yosemite stables to the right and outside it horses milling in a pen, and I thought maybe we shouldn't have aborted that trail in Banff, that I shouldn't have spent a good week before that trip reading about bear attacks—campers dragged from their tents in the fog of the night. *Lie on your stomach, hands gripping the back of the neck, backpack covering the kidneys. Never look the bear in the eye.* And all the attack stats. My husband had said I was good at that: scaring myself.

I glanced at him now, water bottle dangling from his hand. "We're halfway there, aren't we?" I said, but he didn't seem to hear me. Absorbed, I assumed, in his "Yosemite mind," as he liked to call it, he just kept walking while I, beside him, spotted something odd ahead, a circle of shade in the middle of the trail. Slowing down, I looked from the circle to my husband's back, to the horses again, still milling, unperturbed, then back to the circle, where I saw the shape of something now, an outline of an animal, a tall, skinny dog, sitting on its haunches. And my husband, apparently unaware of it, was heading right toward it. Another twenty feet and that would be it. Still, I lagged behind. In the past, I'd mistaken tree trunks for bears and branches for rattlers. I shut my eyes and then opened them again, but nothing had changed, and I knew, just as I'd known in Banff when I'd looked into the woman's face, that trouble was ahead. Scooting up behind my husband, I touched his shoulder. "Lion," I whispered. His head jerked up, and he froze. The animal was sitting stone still at the center of the trail, fixed on the horses, and we, fixed on the lion, watched it, watched until it slowly sank down to its belly and crawled across the trail, into the sunlight, closer to the horses. Its triangular ears, tipped with tufts of hair, were erect, and its tawny coat was spotted.

"There's a cutoff right over there, a few feet ahead. Follow me," my husband said softly, starting to move slowly forward, angling toward the trail's edge, keeping his eye on the lion.

I followed, listening to my own footfall, each scrape of pebble, each snap of twig. Though the sign had said to face the lion, not to run or turn your back, I couldn't help but look over my shoulder. To run back down the trail, back to where it started, the bridge at the base of Yosemite Falls where people were snapping pictures and the great engines of the tour buses were softly rumbling in the parking lot was what I wanted to do, but I felt my husband's hand on my shoulder. "You first," he said.

I peered over the edge, to a short, steep, gravel path, and shook my head. "Down this backward?" One stumble and I knew the lion would be on us.

My husband pointed. "You forward." Then he turned around and pressed his back against mine. "We'll hold each other up."

Squatting low, I inched down, keeping my knees bent, my hips to the ground. Halfway down now, I realized my husband wasn't there, and I stopped and looked back over my shoulder at him still perched at the top of the slope, at the edge, just standing there. Annoyed, I hissed, "What are you doing?"

He twisted back to glance at me, then turned forward again and carefully slid one foot back, then the other, inching backward like a tightrope walker, looking every so often over his shoulder at the ground, then forward again. When he reached me, we moved down the rest of the slope together, back-to-back, his body against mine, until his weight was too much and my foot slipped, and I skidded, fell to my knee, and I slid the rest of the way down.

At the bottom, my husband pulled me up. "You're bleeding," he said.

I looked down at my knee, at the long red scrapes, the bits of gravel stuck to it. Then I looked upslope. "Where is it?"

"Come on." My husband took my hand and pulled me past the stable.

"We better find a ranger," I said.

"What for?"

"We're so close to the village, all these houses." I looked down at the stone chimneys, the steep roofs of the park personnel houses. Behind one, in a backyard, were three little children all crouched in a circle, poking at something with a stick. "What if…" I started to say, but my husband, staring straight ahead, said, "They'll see the sign. It can't get any bigger."

"A sign and a sighting are two different things." I let go of his hand. "Besides, people don't read signs." We stepped onto a service road behind the village.

"We do, don't we?"

"We," I said, taking the water bottle from him, "aren't people." I poured water onto my palm, then splashed it on my knee. It was turning pink and puffy and starting to burn. Handing him the bottle, I said, "I still think we should report it. Those children—they're not going to see any signs. Don't you care?"

"Then you'd better hurry. There's one of your rangers right now, heading for his car."

"Hey!" I shouted, half-running, half-limping. "Lion! Up there!"

The ranger, a heavyset man wearing a beige Yosemite uniform, looked up at me, and then opened his car door. "You don't say."

"We got off trail," I said, "gave it lots of space."

The ranger nodded. "That's probably a good idea." Reaching into his car, he pulled out a pair of sunglasses. "That one's a youngster, a male, seen a couple times before. You're lucky, though." He nodded again. "Getting a look at him. I've worked the park twelve years and never seen one."

"Well, he's probably still up there right now." I glanced back at my husband, who was milling behind me, then back to the ranger, who had gotten into the car and was watching me as if I were the lion. Walking back over to my husband, I said, "I don't think he believed me."

He shrugged. "Forget it. These days rangers spend more time policing people than animals." He started walking between two buildings into the village.

In front of the Ansel Adams Gallery, I sat down on a bench while my husband hunted for something to eat. People, smiling and happy, were making their way from the ranger station to the food concessions—pizza and deli— where rental bikes with clover-shaped seats and pedal brakes were parked in metal stalls. In front of the post office, a stone cottage, a gray-haired man with a blue backpack slipped a postcard in the mailbox. Nearby, a dog, tied to a post, kept barking. A little girl walking with her family tried to pet it, but the dog lunged at her.

"Here," my husband said, handing me a piece of pizza. "You'll feel better."

"Better?" I said. "We could have been killed."

Chuckling, my husband popped open a soda and put it between us. "Look, if the lion wanted to kill you, he would have come up behind you and you wouldn't have known the difference. You wouldn't have heard a thing, and then it would be over."

"What makes you such an expert on lions?" I asked, annoyed all over again.

"I didn't say I was an expert on anything. I just know a few things."

"Who knows what that lion would have done if you'd dawdled there longer." I took a sip of soda and put the can back down. "Just like that guy who kept getting closer and closer to the snake."

"Snake? I thought we were talking about lions." He took a bite of pizza, then picked up the can of soda.

"Last summer, the rattler out at Big Sur all coiled up on the trail. The guy's wife was half hysterical, screaming at her husband to back off. Remember?"

"I remember the woman. I don't remember him getting bit, though."

"That's because we didn't wait around. The woman was getting on your nerves. You walked right past the snake."

"And lived, right?"

"We got lucky," I said.

"Maybe the snake liked us."

"Sure." I laughed. "Snakes love you."

"I mean, the ranger in the parking lot said there were snakes all over the place, and there were warning signs."

"That's true." I looked over at all the buildings, behind them the road where the ranger had been parked. "But I don't get why the ranger here didn't hightail it up to the trail. He'd said he'd never seen a lion before."

"Maybe he didn't want to seem anxious. Maybe he was scared. Like I said, rangers spend more time giving speeding tickets than wrangling with lions."

"But what about those children?"

"It was the horses it was after, and the horses didn't even care. We could have walked right by and kept going."

"Right," I said, rolling my eyes.

My husband stood up and dropped the remains of our lunch in a garbage can. Let's head over to Vernal, join the masses."

"I think we're already among them," I said, rising. Walking back, we passed the post office. The dog, a little poodle, was still there, wagging its tail now though, its owner, kneeling down, untying its leash.

Desert Draw

4:00 p.m. and my husband and I were getting a late start on our hike. We were on our yearly Death Valley trip, maybe our last, since we were thinking of separating, going our own way. This road ended, as they all did, at the mouth of a canyon—today, Desolation Canyon, a hike we'd never done in the many years we'd been coming to the park. Yesterday's hike to Zabriskie Point, one of our favorites, had taken us up to a tourist-ridden area offering hypnotic views of rippling canyons. There, the paved parking lot had been full; here in Desolation Canyon, though, there was no lot, only an old van, burnt orange with tinted windows, parked up against the wall. My husband, after turning off the ignition, opened his book *Hiking California's Death Valley*, on the cover rippling sand dunes, a man hiking across them. "I want to look over the trail description one more time," he said.

I got out, walked toward the van, and then called back to my husband. "You think it's abandoned?" Then I peered over at the trailhead. Rocky, shadeless, it looked as desolate as its namesake. Badwater, Hell's Gate, Devil's Golf Course, the Funeral Mountains—some, attracted by the grim names, came to the park to kill themselves, even whole families, I'd read three nights ago in the *Tehachapi Gazette* when a freak snowstorm up in the mountains had forced us off the road into a dive motel for the night on our way to the park.

But still, I thought as I headed toward the van, it was hard to believe a family would come out here, twenty miles of washboard just to get in. At the van now, I took off my sunglasses, trying to see in.

"Hey," my husband shouted, "what are you doing?" He was out of the car now.

I walked back over to him. "There's a big straw hat in there and a dozen sealed up garbage bags. No seats at all."

My husband pulled our pack out of the car and slung it on his shoulder; then he handed me the water bottle. "You're going to get yourself in trouble one of these days."

Truth was I was already in trouble, my husband thinking I'd cheated on him, but for the sake of the trip we'd called a truce.

"What do you think is in those bags?" I asked, as we headed over to the trail.

"Not what you think. Manson's in prison now, an old man, right? Isn't that what you said?"

"Right. The court reversed his death sentence." That was in the *Gazette* story too, Charles Manson's time in Death Valley, stowed up in the Panamints, up Goler Canyon, at the Barker Ranch, where he'd hatched his plans for the sensational Tate-LaBianca murders some forty years ago. After we'd left Tehachapi, I'd said we could go see the ranch for ourselves, the turn-off for Goler Canyon off the main road into the park.

We walked single file down the narrow trail as it rose and dipped, my husband leading. I stopped for a minute and looked back at the van, still thinking of Manson, the school bus he drove up Goler Canyon, his followers in it. He hadn't actually committed the murders but instead sent his followers—alienated, drug-crazed runaways he'd collected, brainwashed. I turned back around and started up the trail again, but my husband was already out of sight. He'd wait up, though, I knew, so I kept walking, listening to the ground crunch beneath my boots, the sky above, blue, unforgiving. Already hot, I wiped my forehead and then heard footsteps, foot-dragging behind me. Pausing, I looked back. A man in a gray T-shirt and white pants was coming toward me, a tripod under his arm, a small, square pack on his back. Gut hanging over his waist, he could have been any man, middle-aged, out of shape. I lifted my hand, but he didn't seem to see me. I turned and started walking again. But then I heard footfall right behind me, the man somehow having caught up with me. As he veered slightly around me, head down, passing, I caught the side of his face. It was flushed and puffy, and he was breathing heavily. Stopping, I watched him for a minute, hauling his tripod, its dark legs dragging behind him. Yesterday, up at Zabriskie Point were all sorts of tripods, armchair photographers behind them. I started walking again, up ahead my husband's familiar shape coming into view.

Leaning against a rock, he lifted his hand.

"Did you see that weird guy?" I asked, coming up alongside him.

"With the camera gear and strange pack. Yeah," he said.

"God knows what he thought of ours." I glanced over at it on the ground, a ratty thing we'd patched up over the years, lightweight and flexible, perfect desert material. I peered up the trail, a fork ahead, to the left a wide wash, to the right a narrow one.

"Which way are we going?" I asked.

My husband lifted the pack. "Your choice."

"So where do you suppose he came from, the man," I said, as we headed to the fork. "I didn't hear a car come up the road."

My husband shrugged. "Anywhere. Park's full of unmarked roads."

At the fork now, we stopped. Above us on a small outcropping of rock between the washes was the man again, tripod still under his arm. His hand above his brow, he squinted down at us. "Hey, which way?"

I took off my sunglasses and looked up at him, his face still red, his shirt now stained with sweat.

"Makes no difference," my husband said. "Trail's round trip."

"That so? Well thank you very much." Turning, he scrambled forward, dragging the tripod.

"Now why'd you tell him that?" I whispered, though this wasn't the first time we'd run into a solo hiker, always men, lonely sorts, coming up behind us, wanting some company. Harmless. But we'd never had anyone backtrack on us, *then* get friendly. Plus, he had no water.

My husband shrugged. "We can take the other wash a ways. Or we can just turn back. It doesn't look like the most promising trail anyway."

I peered down the narrow wash, the man out of sight now.

My husband drank from the water bottle.

"I can carry the pack," I said, taking it from him. As we walked, I unzipped the front pocket, slid my hand in, feeling for the pocketknife we always carried.

"So what else did that Manson article say?" my husband asked.

"The Barker Ranch, where the gang stayed. There was a picture of it. Pleasant-looking. One story. Stone. That's where the police found Manson. A small guy. Hiding in a cabinet under the sink. Now people camp there. Can't seem to stay away. The Park Service is thinking of razing it."

My husband stopped and wiped his forehead, no shade in sight. "Okay, I think I've seen enough. Let's head back. Cut our losses."

I looked up the trail at the parched, colorless landscape. "Hold on," I said, spotting an opening in the canyon wall. We'd scrambled up chutes before, vertical openings, the result of erosion, even though they could be dangerous.

The Zabriskie Point hike had lots of them. I peered up the chute. "What do you think?" I asked.

"I don't know," my husband said. "Looks steep. I'd better go first. I'll call if I think it's passable." He started pulling himself up.

"Okay," I said, though I didn't like being left behind, especially here so far from the main road. "Call me," I shouted up as he climbed, the chute swallowing him up. Stepping back, I drank from the water bottle. Then, looking for some shade, I saw about ten feet up trail a small apron, a shadow extending out from the canyon wall. Something was in it, though, lying down, and as I took a few steps toward it I saw the thick curved horns of a ram and stopped. I'd heard they were in the park, but I'd never seen one. I expected it to bolt, but it just lay there, placidly peering at me as I stood in the sun sweating. I ran back to the chute. "Hey!" You up there?" I shouted. I dropped the pack and pulled myself up, started climbing, the walls closing around me. But my feet slipped and I stopped, worried about getting back down, and, crouching, rotated, and slid back out, using my palms as brakes. Back in the wash, I brushed my hands off. They burned a little, scraped up and bleeding.

"You see that bighorn?"

I swung around. The man had glasses on now, thick ones making his eyes blurry. He laid his tripod down.

I took a step back, trying to appear nonchalant.

He nodded toward the chute. "Your husband up there?"

"You get its picture? The ram," I asked.

"I got my shot. Looks like you hurt yourself there."

I looked at my hands, at the narrow cuts.

"Let me fix you up," the man said, reaching behind for his pack.

"That's all right." I lifted my pack, reaching in, feeling for the knife.

The man turned back around. "Whatever you say." He lifted the tripod as if he were going to leave but instead started opening it, spreading its legs. "Now no need to be afraid. Your husband, he'll be fine if you…" He took a few steps toward me and then stopped. "Now what do you have there?" he asked, as I struggled to get the knife open. But the knife slipped out of my hand, falling not far from me, glinting in the sun. We both lunged for it, and then I heard a dull thud, the man hitting his head on a rock protruding from the wall. On the ground now, on his stomach, he was groaning. A trickle of blood ran down the side of his head. Then suddenly sand and pebbles rushed down the chute, and then my husband, landing on his feet. Looking from the man, to me, then down to the knife, my husband asked, "What's going on here?" He picked up the knife.

The man, rolling onto his back, grimaced. "Your wife. She tried to kill me."

"That's not true. I didn't do anything. He came after me."

My husband walked over to the tripod, beside it, the man's pack, and unzipped it.

I squatted down beside him.

"What if he has a gun?" I asked.

"A gun?" My husband looked back at the man.

Sitting up now, he was holding his head, rocking back and forth.

Wallet, lenses, boxes of film, Band-Aids, a stack of pictures, women, shot from behind, shoulders down, my husband leafing through.

"Shouldn't we check his ID?" I asked.

"I don't want to know who he is," my husband said, putting everything back, zipping up the pack. "Let's get out of here. We're not far from the trailhead. Come on." My husband grabbed our pack.

The man was looking over at us now. Beads of sweat covered his forehead. He was still bleeding. "You're just going to leave me?"

"Don't say anything," my husband whispered. "He's not hurt that bad. He'll get out himself. Let's go." He took my hand, and we started hiking out. I looked back again. The man hadn't moved, but now he was shouting at us. "You won't get away with this!"

"Get away with what?" my husband asked. "Did you stab him?"

"Are you crazy?" I said. "Did you see those pictures?"

"Come on," my husband said.

We started walking faster and faster until we were running, sprinting. After we came around a curve, my face burning, I said, "Wait," and we slowed down. Bent over, sweating, I tried to catch my breath. I started feeling dizzy.

"Look," my husband said. "Something just ran across the trail."

"What?" I felt myself go cold.

"Over there."

We went over to the canyon wall. There, a large, tufted bird with enormous feet and black-ringed eyes was whipping a mouse against a rock, the rock speckled with blood.

"Roadrunner," my husband said. "They break all the bones, swallow their prey whole."

"Hey! Wait up!" The man, half-walking, half-limping, was coming toward us, dragging his tripod.

"I don't believe it," I said.

My husband pulled me back on the trail, and we started running again, not stopping until we reached the mouth of the canyon. I wiped the hair out of my eyes. Sweat was running down my back; my shirt clung to me. I drank from the water bottle, thinking of the ram, cool in its apron of shade, its glassy eyes taking me in, and I shivered. The wind, as it often did late afternoon, had picked up, was whooshing through the canyon. I handed my husband the water bottle. "We must have lost him this time," I said.

My husband took a sip and then shook his head. "Don't bet on it. Wouldn't surprise me if he's already back."

I put my hands on my hips. "That's impossible. Are you trying to scare me?"

"I thought you liked being scared. Isn't that why you wanted to go to the Manson place?"

"I was just kidding about that. You'd need a winch to get up there." Confused, I looked at my husband.

He walked toward the car.

"I didn't stab him, you know. He came after me. And I didn't cheat on you," I shouted. But my husband kept walking. Sighing, I turned around, taking one last look, the wind lifting the sand, swirling it up into miniature tornadoes, tiny ghosts traveling across the landscape.

Hurt

It could have been a picture-perfect trip thanks to the big water—the massive waterfalls and swollen river—the result of a record-breaking winter, all of it on the local news, driving people who'd never been to Yosemite to Yosemite. But a week or so before my husband and I had made our own trip to the park, we'd heard that a driver going off the road drowned in the Merced; a child climbing the rocks above the base of Yosemite Falls slipped; a woman crossing the Wapama Falls footbridge got swept off. Every year people died in the park; Yosemite veterans, we knew this. Fortunately, though, we'd never gotten hurt, not even on this trip, where water washing over the steep, rocky trails made footing treacherous. But then, an hour or so before we'd planned to leave to make the drive home, we'd decided to take a quick, late-afternoon bike ride on the paved trail to Mirror Lake, and that's when everything had changed.

Driving through the park exit gates now, my husband checked his rearview again and then sped up.

I looked too. I couldn't help it, all his checking making me anxious. "There's no one back there," I said. "Just the bikes." My back tire, still intact, was spinning; my mangled front tire, though, would need replacing.

My husband took a deep breath and lifted his hands off the wheel, then dropped them back down, tightening his grip. He was still upset, even though he hadn't actually seen my bike collision this morning, just heard the bloodcurdling scream, what had made him stop, turn his bike around. But by then it was too late. The girl, hurtling down the hill, had already gone over her handlebars while I'd flown off my bike backwards. By the time I'd gathered myself and managed to get off my back and on my feet, everyone, all the walkers and riders on the trail, had vanished.

"Easy does it," I said. "We don't want to get a ticket."

"Let's just skip Hetch Hetchy. Head home."

All the years we'd been trying to see Hetch Hetchy, something had always stopped us, forcing us to deadhead home. "Let's go anyway. Check out Wapama Falls. It's such a short drive in," I said, even though I knew it sounded childish, even callous, given what had happened, the girl, never regaining consciousness, airlifted out. I, on the other hand, had been more fortunate, though the paramedic, lifting up the back of my shirt, seemed puzzled that I had no cracked ribs, no abrasions. Had I hit my head, he'd asked, seeming annoyed, agitated for some reason. He smelled bad too; an artery in his neck was throbbing. I couldn't stop staring at it. Now though I felt better, my hands no longer shaking, everything under control.

"How's your foot? What did the paramedic say?" my husband said.

I looked down at it, the gauze wrapped around my ankle, over my Achilles, blood still oozing through. "They wanted to put in a stitch or two, to close the wound. But I don't feel anything. I'm fine."

"Once all the adrenalin wears off, you're probably going to feel a lot of things. What about the girl? I saw you kneeling beside her."

I shook my head. "She looked like she was sleeping. Her eyelashes were fluttering. There was no blood." The image of her came back to me—arms flung over her head, dark hair spread out in a halo, somehow her flip-flops still on, toenails painted. "He was caressing her cheek, talking to her so sweetly. The boyfriend," I said.

My husband slowed down. "Her boyfriend?"

"I assume that's who he was, the guy beside her. He was on one of those rental bikes like hers. The clover-shaped seats. The pedal brakes."

My husband slowed down and put on his signal. "You're lucky he didn't kill you. I mean she might be brain damaged. Isn't that what the paramedic said? Are you sure you didn't cross the yellow line?" He cut the wheel, and we started down the road to Hetch Hetchy.

Sighing, I took off my sunglasses and looked out my window at the dense forest, the thick boughs, not one tree withered or dying.

"We won't be able to stay long. It's already past 5:00," he said. "The gates there close early."

"Why? Is that when the spirits come out?"

"More like the city of San Francisco. They own the dam, I think."

"I meant the animals. When they flooded the valley, they must have all drowned. Isn't that what the Indians believe?"

"Who knows what the Indians believe."

"There's a lodge around here too, isn't there?" I said.

"Up ahead. At the clearing." My husband slowed down again as we passed small shingled cottages, some run-down, some newer looking, and then a larger building, in front of it a dirt parking lot, lots of cars in it, a sign arcing over it: The Hetch Hetchy Lodge.

"Where is everyone?" I asked.

"Back at their campsites or in the restaurant, eating." My husband sped up again.

Fifteen minutes later we pulled into a lot. Here, out of the forest, it was lighter. Below us was the dam, a massive cement structure. I put my sunglasses back on. My husband, out of the car, went around back to lock our bikes and grab a water bottle while I stayed put, easing my foot back into a sandal. The laceration wasn't my only injury. The puncture wound above it had already stopped bleeding, though. My husband came around my side and opened the door. "Why don't we just check out the dam and then head back?" He looked over his shoulder at the road.

I got out. "Remember, I was going uphill. She crossed the yellow line. That's what I told them. The rangers. I have no idea why they didn't believe me." I took a few steps, testing my foot. Then, as we headed down to the dam, we could hear the Tuolumne thundering down. On the crest we peered over the wall into the white torrent, the abyss, and then we went over to the other side, where the dark, placid water sat, a liquid forest, a graveyard of animals, three hundred feet beneath.

"Where's the trail?" I asked.

"Through there." At the end of the overpass was a dark, cave-like tunnel. My husband took my hand, and we started toward it.

At the entrance I could feel the cool, damp air, could hear water dripping. I took off my sunglasses and slid them in my pocket. "Did you bring a flashlight?" I asked, worried about stepping in a puddle or stumbling over a rock.

"It's not that long."

"I hope there's no rattlers in here," I said, my voice echoing as we made our way through.

"Maybe frogs or newts."

"Newts? Isn't that the stuff of witchcraft?"

"Actually, they're the stuff of science. They can grow back missing limbs and organs." He pointed to the exit, the circle of light. "Okay, here we go."

Out of the tunnel now, I slipped my sunglasses on again. "That was weird."

"No weirder than the rest of the day. Sure you want to do this? We can come back another time."

"Let's go in a ways. The falls aren't that far, are they?" The flat trail seemed tame enough, though, shrubs and trees upslope, the reservoir downslope. I started walking.

My husband looked down at my foot. "Why didn't you get the stitches?"

I shrugged. "If I'd been hurt worse, maybe I would have. Maybe then they'd believe me."

"Maybe you're hurt worse than you think."

I looked down, my thighs now bruising.

"You must have gotten tangled up into your bike."

"I still don't feel a thing. Not even when I landed. I wish I had."

The trail continued along the reservoir but then started winding in toward a sloping, rocky meadow split by a stream.

"This probably wouldn't exist during a normal season," my husband said. "We'll have to figure out where to cross." He walked around. "Over here." He hopped across a few rocks to the other side, and I followed, though my foot, stiff now, slipped, the gauze getting wet and muddy.

"Are we almost there?" I asked.

"Listen."

I could hear water in the distance. We started toward it, and around the corner the falls suddenly appeared, a torrent of white water tumbling over jutting rocks, sheets of water pouring across the bridge.

"Jesus, no wonder that woman got swept away," I said.

"There's no way we're crossing, not with your foot."

I looked down at it, the gauze now reddish-black, my foot not only stiff but starting to ache now.

My husband drank from the water bottle and then handed it to me. "Let's go. We don't want to get stuck here."

We started back, my husband ahead of me, walking briskly. Waiting at the stream, he helped me cross, and then he left me behind again. But a few minutes later he stopped and turned. "Can you walk any faster?"

I tried to speed up but was limping now. Worried, I wanted to stop, unwrap the gauze, but instead I said, "I'm fine." Then I spotted something ahead on the trail. "Hey, look at that." Hetch Hetchy was supposed to be full of deer and what preyed on them—mountain lions.

"It's just a fawn," my husband said. "Come on." He took my hand. "She'll move." And as we got closer, she suddenly sprang upslope and started chewing on a shrub.

"Mama must be nearby, "I said.

"Probably."

We kept walking, and a few minutes later I looked back again. "She's following us."

"She'll turn back."

"But what if she doesn't?"

"She's too small to hurt anyone."

We kept on. My husband dropped my hand, but he slowed down every so often, waiting for me. Nearing the tunnel, we both stopped again. The fawn, closer now, was nosing the ground, peeking up at us every so often.

"She's lovely," I said.

"Probably orphaned," my husband said.

"It means something, doesn't it, to be followed by deer?"

"Can you run a little? Let's try to lose her."

I started half jogging, half limping, but now the pain had grown sharp. Fortunately, though, the tunnel was in sight.

"What if she follows us in?" I said, the fawn now only some ten feet behind us, craning her neck toward us.

"She won't."

"We can't just leave her here. It'll be dark soon."

"Are you sure you didn't hit your head?"

"But what if she goes in?"

"She can always go back."

We headed in. It was much darker now. I could hardly make out my husband as he moved ahead of me. Veering over to the side, I felt my way along the cold, damp wall, and started shivering. When I got out, my husband said, "Five minutes before the gates close."

"We should report it," I said, as we crossed the dam and approached the parking lot.

"Right. And then what?" He unlocked the doors.

I put on my seat belt and peered over at the overpass. In the oncoming darkness, it seemed to glow white. As my husband backed out, I turned on the radio, knowing I'd get nothing but static, then switched it off.

"We'll stop at the lodge so you can clean up your foot. Aspirin's in the glove compartment. Take three. There's more gauze too." My husband turned on his headlights, and we started back down the road, the forest closing in on us again. Ten minutes later a car passed us. "Where do you suppose they're going?" I asked. Then we saw the lodge ahead, a stand of Christmas lights blinking across the main building. The lot was packed, but one car was pulling out, and my husband took the space. As I got out, I heard voices singing in the distance. *Row, row, row your boat…* "Where's that coming from?" I asked, but my husband was already at the building, holding the door open. Inside, an old woman stood behind the counter.

"Sold out," she said, as we approached. "Them religious nuts. Out there on a retreat."

"We'd just like to use your restroom," my husband said. "My wife's injured." He looked down at my foot.

The old woman leaned over the counter and tried to look too. "Down the hall."

In the bathroom I stuck my foot in the sink and unwrapped the gauze. The wound looked larger now, more torn open. I turned on the water, watching blood and mud swirl down the drain, everything around the wound now tender and swollen. After rewrapping my foot, I swallowed the aspirin. Then I went back out, passing the check-in counter, and stepped through the door.

"How is it?" my husband asked.

"Not bad," I said, knowing if I said anything else he'd want to stop at a hospital, an ER, on the way home.

"You got lucky," my husband said.

"What do you mean? That I didn't land on my head like she did?"

From behind us the door suddenly burst open. "Hey you two. Just got a cancellation. Want it?" the old woman said.

"Thank you," I said, "but we're not staying."

"We'll think about it," my husband said.

"Well, don't think too long." The old woman went back inside.

"Maybe we should," my husband said. "Four hours back. It's going to be uncomfortable for you. Who knows what else you hurt."

"I just took the aspirin." I looked across the lot to the dark road and forest on the other side. *Merrily, merrily, merrily, merrily life is but a dream…* I thought of the fawn we'd left behind. "You think she'll make it?"

My husband sighed. "You mean the girl? She's young, right? It would be different if she were old."

The Fugitive Widow

Grief (joys,) joy grieves on slender accident.
This world is not for aye, nor 'tis not strange
That even our loves should with our fortunes change;

—Hamlet

Retired six months, Addison was sixty-five, and he'd never been a hiker. He was a putterer. He puttered in the garden, puttered on the golf course, and puttered in his job. An insurance salesman, he was never going to become vice president, and as a husband he'd never swept Delia off her feet nor she him, as far as she could tell. And that was all right, all that sweeping was just Hollywood anyway. Anyone selling life insurance long enough knew there were few perfect marriages, enough husbands secretly taking their wives off the policy and putting their mistresses on. Now Delia and Addison were on their first post-retirement trip to Death Valley, a place Addison always wanted to see. At dawn today they'd watch the sun rise over Zabriskie Point, lighting up the badlands, a series of undulating, veined mountains that to Delia looked like the backs of enormous whales rising out of the earth. Up north in Modesto, where they lived, everything was still green from the early spring rains, the Delta flush with water and long-necked egrets, but here in

Death Valley everything seemed parched, lifeless to Delia, even though the ranger brochure said there was life, lots of it, if you only looked for it.

Then after lunch, they went to Badwater, another popular spot, 282 feet below sea level, where they walked across the blinding white salt flats, Addison insisting he saw through his binoculars a cabin where the salt flats met the mountains and wanted to walk out to it. But Delia knew those mountains weren't close at all, just a mirage, and told him so, the heat making Addison partly insane. He wasn't the only one, of course. She'd heard stories about people going to the desert to find God and such, and, though she herself wasn't religious or inclined to epiphany, she wasn't wholly inhospitable to the idea. After Badwater, the plan was to drive back to the room, wash up, relax, then go for an early dinner. But now, driving back, Addison's hands suddenly flew off the wheel as they passed a second sign for Golden Canyon. "There it is again! The Manly Beacon! The Manly Beacon!"

"The Manly what?" Delia said.

"Up at Zabriskie. We saw it this morning from the other side. Don't you remember?"

Delia peered at the stretch of mountains.

"The whitish one sticking up there like a fin," Addison said.

"Why's it called that? Doesn't look very manly to me." Delia chuckled.

"It's named after the man who rescued gold rush families trying to cross the valley. Charles Manly. A bunch of things are named after him like Lake Manly, but that's all dried up now."

They passed a sign for Golden Canyon.

Addison slowed down, turning on his blinker. "That's where the trail starts to get there, and I'm going to take it." He turned into the lot and pulled into the only empty spot.

"What? Now? You're supposed to take these trails in the morning, Addison."

"It's only a couple of miles. An hour and a half tops. Look at all those people."

They were milling at the mouth of the canyon, some even older looking than them, but Delia couldn't tell if they'd just come back or were starting.

"You can go too, Delia," Addison said.

"Me? I still don't think it's a good idea. You've never hiked before. You don't even have a map."

"Golden Canyon to the Manly Beacon out Gower Gulch and back around to Golden Canyon. Round trip. Two hours. I read about it in the ranger brochure last night." Addison reached back grabbing two water bottles and his hat, a floppy thing with a Death Valley logo, a skull and crossbones on it, he'd bought their first day in at the general store. He put it on, tightening the drawstring under his chin.

"But Addison…why don't you wait till tomorrow?" Delia said, though she hated to keep discouraging him. Without hobbies, retirement would be hard on him.

"Tomorrow's golf and the Ubehebe Crater," he said, opening his door and getting out.

Reluctantly, Delia slid behind the wheel. "Promise me you'll turn back if you get too hot or run out of water. I'll pick you up right here. Two hours, right?"

Addison leaned into the window and gave her a kiss on the cheek. "Promise." Then he headed toward the canyon, through the people hovering there, eventually disappearing.

After backing out, Delia pulled onto the main road, and was at their motel after a few minutes. For the next two hours she sat on the balcony writing out postcards and reading a book about roadrunners she'd picked up at the ranger station. Without the shade of the overhang, though, it would have been much too hot to even do this. She tried not to worry about Addison, the heat here being at its worst in the afternoons, but later when she went back to Golden Canyon Addison wasn't there. Standing beside the car, Delia checked her watch. Fortunately, Addison had left his bin-oculars behind and so she scanned the ridge he'd said he'd be coming back along, below it a steep drop-off. Then she looked over at the canyon entrance again where people were still gathered and thought about asking if anyone had seen him. But what he was wearing—the blue-striped or the beige polo with the alligator on the front pocket? She got back in the car, out of the sun. It felt like triple digits, the heat building up, the ground and rock holding on to it, a strange kind of heat that didn't immediately bowl you over but crept up on you. In the car she lifted the binoculars, training them again on the ridge again. She could go skirt it herself, but she knew most of the trail had to be inside the canyon, where it would be even hotter, and she wasn't so surefooted, and of course now she wondered if she'd just gotten it wrong, if the Zabriskie lot where they'd been this morning was the pick-up point. But didn't he say round trip? She waited another ten minutes and drove up there anyway. Where was he? Bewildered, she stood beside the car again, the Zabriskie lot much larger, more crowded, cars jockeying for spots. Beside hers was a black Jeep, Desert Madness stenciled on it, two young, blond couples behind it chattering excitedly in German. Their hiking boots and socks were covered in dust.

"Excuse me," Delia said, "I wonder if you've seen my husband. 65 years old. Hiking alone. Two bottles of water. Wearing a funny hat."

They all looked at each other and started laughing, and then one of the young men said, "No, no one like that."

"But we really weren't looking, were we?" one of the young women said, looking very serious now. "Maybe he's up at the viewpoint."

Delia walked up there. It was just as crowded as it had been at sunrise, plenty of tourists snapping pictures or bent over tripods, children chasing each other. Trying to think what to do, she sat down on the stone wall that arced around and peered at the many mountains, each folding back behind one another. And the Manly Beacon sticking up in the sky. That ridiculous fin. Delia returned to the lot and drove back to the motel. In the room she picked up the phone. "My husband… He… Addison Macy…" She hung up. The reception here was bad. The first day they'd arrived a wind storm had knocked the power out for a few hours. Then the phone rang, startling her.

"This is the front desk. I'm afraid we got disconnected. How can I help you?" Delia heard the operator say as her eye landed on Addison's gold watch resting on the nightstand. Well, no wonder he didn't show up. "Oh, I'm sorry. It was a mistake." She hung up. Why hadn't he taken it? Why hadn't she reminded him to take it? She picked it up, big, heavy, worthless, watching the second hand make its way around, wobbling a little, the culmination of his career, insuring against catastrophe. Delia got up and walked out onto the balcony. Was she making something out of nothing? Shouldn't she just drive back to Golden Canyon? Likely he was just running late, was waiting for her wondering where *she* was. She peered at the enormous tree some twenty feet from her balcony, a massive tamarisk offering an apron of shade to a crow on the ground beneath it. Last night that very tree had kept her awake, its brittle limbs creaking pitifully as another windstorm had swept through, Addison snoring through the whole thing. She looked back into the room, Addison's golf clubs standing up in the corner, the woods and irons, all brand new. He'd played only once; he was taking lessons. She went back in and picked up the phone, but then there was a knock at the door, and she hurried to it, thinking he'd found a way back. But why wasn't he using his key?

"Good afternoon, ma'am. Are you Mrs. Macy?"

Delia looked over his uniform, the khaki pants, the long-sleeved shirt, the stiff broad-brimmed hat that sat just above his eyes and felt her stomach flutter.

"I'm Ranger Fowles. May I come in?"

Delia walked back into the room and sat on the bed.

"The front desk just informed me that you called. That you seemed upset. Are you aware, Mrs. Macy, that your husband was hiking in Golden Canyon?"

"I was supposed to pick him up about two hours ago, but he never showed up. I was about to go back…"

"But why did you hang up? Why didn't you report it?"

"I just assumed I got the time wrong. Or he did." She looked down, trying to think of what to say, and then back up at the ranger. "I mean I tried."

"Tried?"

"To call, but I didn't want to embarrass him. He was so determined… You see, he just retired. He sold insurance. And now—how did you know he was hiking there?"

"Mrs. Macy, a man was found at the base of the Manly Beacon."

"That's where he said the trail went. Up to the top, I think. To that fin."

"There is no trail to the top of the Manly Beacon, Mrs. Macy. You have to scramble to get up there." The ranger took off his hat and held it against his chest. "This man—we think he may have slipped, though there was no obvious injury to his body. Or maybe a medical event preceded this—heart attack or heat stroke. The autopsy should determine that."

"But that can't be my husband." Delia looked over at Addison's watch. "It was only two hours ago—you mean he's dead?"

"We checked his ID. He had his wallet. In these temperatures, in the canyons, it can happen suddenly. No one's immune. He'd run out of water. I'm sorry for your loss, Mrs. Macy. Is there anyone I can call? Children?"

"Addison—dead? Are you sure?"

"Some hikers found him. He'll be transported to Bishop for the autopsy."

On the drive into Death Valley she and Addison had stopped there at a Bishop bakery, a million tourists and all the disgusting pastries, but then afterward, leaving the bakery, the most incredible thing, a duck sitting on her eggs in a planter right by the side of the road.

"Mrs. Macy, are you sure there isn't anyone I can call?"

Delia shook her head.

"There was a camera," the ranger said. "We're getting the film developed. We'll need to meet again. Tomorrow. Around 3:00 pm. I'll come to your room." He handed her a card. "If you need anything tonight. Again, please accept my condolences. I'll see myself out."

Delia laid the card beside the phone. There were children, and they'd need to be called—others too, but what was she supposed to say? "Your father went out on a hike and got himself killed. I dropped him off and let him go." *Poor Addison. Not retired a year. What a shame.* What people would say. Or maybe they might blame her. But the old rarely got blamed, age making them less culpable.

Suddenly tired, she lay down on the bed and let her eyes shut. Just a nap and all would return to normal. In would walk a sweaty, sunburned Addison, excited, exhausted, T-shirt soaked in sweat, sneakers and socks coated in dust. A few scrapes maybe. "You wouldn't believe it, Delia…it was hard… but I made it. Can you believe it?"

When Delia opened her eyes though, a luminous silver light shone through the sliding glass door. She looked at the clock; she'd slept a long time. She went out on the balcony, the warm night air wrapping around her, the enormous tamarisk, ghostly in the moonglow, and then shifting her gaze she spotted another tamarisk, a much smaller one in the distance, a boy, maybe a teenager, shirtless and pale, barefooted, circling around it. Hands gesticulating, mouth moving, head bobbing, he seemed to be talking to himself. Then he started skipping, then leaping, then sprinting, suddenly freezing mid stride then unfreezing, repeating the whole bizarre pattern over and over as he kept going round the tree. Delia watched him for a while, thinking how odd, how queer, this boy, a human merry-go-round, until she could no longer stand it and went in and turned on the lights.

DELIA HAD LAIN AWAKE the rest of the night and by morning still hadn't called anyone. Frankly she didn't see any rush. Why bring misery any sooner than need be? Why ever bring it? And in the end she knew her daughters wouldn't blame her, their aging mother, in shock, alone, in the middle of nowhere. Who would expect her to act rationally? Who would blame her for letting her headstrong husband set out on a deadly hike? Their youngest son, only an hour or two away, a blackjack dealer in Vegas, but who was always at odds with Addison, forgoing college for a pointless life in Vegas, would be too bereft with his own guilt, too dis-combobulated, to blame her, no father left to please. Still, looking over at the phone now, she expected to see the red light blinking, panicked messages piling up. That she could keep such a thing secret, even for a day, that she could pick up the phone and call her children and say, "We're having such a good time we're thinking of extending our trip longer. Maybe another week" seemed impossible. She peered over at Addison's suitcase, propped open on the floor, all his things in it. Nothing out of place.

She got dressed and went out on the balcony. Early, it was pleasantly cool, the sky pale blue. She looked over to that tamarisk tree where that boy had been last night on his mad journey, and then went back in, catching herself in the dresser mirror. Usually she didn't bother looking at herself; no one else did. But now she tried to fix herself, her hair all mashed down on one side from sleep, still a lot of it, though mostly gray. Her eyes were puffy and disappearing yet still very blue, blue, blue. Blue as the desert sky. She put on her sunglasses and grabbed her bag. Outside on the landing of the stairs she peered at the parking lot, wondering if anyone could tell that she was the woman with the dead husband, the one who'd let her husband foolishly disappear into a sweltering canyon, the fugitive widow racing off to the Ubehebe Crater, the very trip she and Addison had planned for today after what should have been his early round of golf.

In the car, she drove out of the lot and onto the main road, an hour or so later arriving at the west side of the park, the weather there anything but placid, the wind gusting and loud. *Like Jupiter, where the wind can blast for a hundred years straight,* Addison had read aloud from some travel book, its warning about this spot. Then, she assumed it was just hyperbole. And so, parked below the rim now, she sat in her car, wondering what to do, if she should get out or just how she'd get out. Then some T.V. show, a documentary, she and Addison had watched together came back to her—*The Warden's Wife*—a true life mystery about a prison warden's wife kidnapped by an escapee, a murderer, both found ten years later living happily together under an alias, on a chicken farm in Kansas. Had she really been kidnapped, or had she gone willingly? Addison said kidnapped, but Delia was sure they'd been in love from the get-go, and as it turned out, the escapee, turning out not to be so bad, eventually became a celebrated artist, how he got found out.

The wind finally lulling, Delia pushed the door open and quickly shut it. Two cars in the crater's lot and one park service Jeep, she felt a little more confident straying out. If she had to, she'd just turn back, no interest in dying in order to achieve some feat. But as she climbed up a short incline to the rim, the wind started up again, pushing her sideways, blowing gravel. Hunched over, she pushed forward to the edge where she peered over the edge to a hole, a giant bowl with rocky black walls, over 600 feet deep, Addison had told her, a few scraggy green mesquite bushes growing from its rusty bottom. Then, mixed into the wind's roar, Delia thought she heard high-pitched screams, and looking to her left, spotted a couple in flip-flops, arms raised above their heads in surrender, hurtling down into the crater on a steep rocky trail, the woman's hair flying up behind her like a dark cape, the man at her heels.

IN THE MOTEL ROOM, Delia showered off the desert grit. Out of the bathroom and at the sink, she peered at Addison's toiletry bag. Unzipping it, she pulled out his razor, floss, a small pair of scissors, two topaz pill bottles, and then she unzipped the other side—eyedrops, toothpaste, mouthwash, among other things. So neat—the dry side and the wet side. She, on the other hand, just threw everything—dry, wet, and everything in between—in one bag. After she got dressed, there was a knock at the door.

"Good afternoon, Mrs. Macy."

Delia took her place on the bed beside the nightstand.

"We're still waiting on the autopsy results. In the meantime we were able to develop the pictures… Only eight on the roll. Nothing unusual. Places you visited before. He laid them out on the dresser, and Delia got up and looked.

"You in front of Mushroom Rock. Several at Badwater. These look like the motel grounds. Salt Creek here."

"That's only seven." Delia said. "Is that the eighth in your hand?"

"Of himself. He managed somehow… But I think it's better to remember people as they were."

"As they were? You mean alive?"

"It's his face. The camera right on him. It might not look like him."

Delia reached out for the picture, and, looking at it, she cringed, Addison's face a pale, round blur, his eyes bulging. "Did he suffer?"

He crossed his arms and looked away from her. "I doubt it. He wouldn't have been conscious long."

Delia handed him back the picture. She knew he was lying, she knew enough about heat stroke, if that's what did it, to know it wasn't a quick, peaceful death. "There were so many people at the trail when I dropped him off. How come no one saw him? I mean he must have been struggling before…"

"He was off trail, scrambling. Down on the ground he might not have been easy to spot. Anyway, I'll be back tomorrow with the results of the autopsy report. The front desk told me you're booked through the end of the week. Are you planning to stay that whole time?"

"I don't see how I can leave. Not without Addison."

"We can help you make arrangements to transport him, but we can talk about that later. If you're children are coming in…we can arrange rooms."

"Did I say I had children?"

"I'm sorry. Thought you had. Well, if you need anything don't hesitate to call… I'm sure your husband was a good man."

Delia sat back down on the bed and sighed. "He was a hard worker. A good provider. I, on the other hand, only raised children, so I already knew there was no purpose in life. No life after life. Just life."

Safe

Five hours into our escape, my husband and I pulled into Bridgeport, 8,000 feet up in the Sierras. Earlier, a little after dusk, we'd seen cows, or the shadows of them, moving slowly across the meadows. But once in town it was too dark to see anything but the dull, fluorescent strip of motels, gas stations, and the brick town hall. Come morning we'd see the tall, snow-capped mountains rising up around the town and, if we were lucky, blue sky. We'd been here many times before—a stop-off on the way to the desert—but this time was different. This was no vacation. It was cold, far colder than we'd expected. At the edge of town, my husband turned into the Bridgeport Inn, pulling up beside the office. I peered out my window at the place, most of its rooms dark, the empty pool, lit by two spotlights, peeling. Come summer, the pool filled, it was a pretty place. Now, early March, still the edge of winter, the motel looked run down, an unhappy place in the middle of nowhere. Or maybe I was just tired, not just from the drive but from months of madness, and I felt guilty boarding our cats. Little cages in a back room of a vet clinic. Still, they'd be safe. No one could get to them.

"Hey, are you coming?" My husband, out of the car now, leaned back in, his door still open. His eyes looked blood-shot, his hair a little grayer. We'd both lost weight.

I opened my door and got out. Before coming around the car, I looked over my shoulder at the road and beyond the road into the darkness half expecting the darkness to take shape.

"There's nothing out there," my husband said, holding the office door open.

"I know," I said, stepping in, taking in the dimly lit room, a coffee maker and Styrofoam cups on a table alongside the wall, the check-in counter across from it, and behind the counter an open door to living quarters. Inside there a T.V. flashed; orange goldfish swam in a large tank. The rest of the office, which I'd seen before, opened into another larger room, a mini museum of glass-encased Indian relics, mounted on the walls, a wooden sled, a rifle, and a deer head. It was dark in there now though. My husband, at the counter, rang the bell. A man in a plaid flannel shirt and jeans padded out in his socks and yawned. We knew him, of course, though never asked his name, and he seemed no different than last year, amiable, maybe a little scattered as if he'd accidentally wandered into his own motel. It was we who were differ-ent—more serious than usual, desperate looking maybe, and I worried he'd notice. People in small towns always noticed and sometimes cared.

"Well, hello, folks. Was just getting ready to close things up." He put on a pair of gold-rimmed glasses and looked at us curiously. "You two come up every year, don't you, but this year seems earlier." He started flipping though some index cards.

"No reservation this time," my husband said. "Do you have a room for tonight?" He pulled his wallet out.

"Maybe two nights," I said. "I take it you're not that busy."

"Just our local deer hunters now. You can have as many nights as you like." He looked at me and chuckled.

I must have been grimacing.

"No fan of hunters, eh?" He slid the credit card through and punched in some numbers.

"Or dead deer," I said. We'd seen them all stiff tied to flatbeds or stacked atop another in town on the sidewalks.

"Me neither. That one over there." He cocked his head toward the dark part of the office. "Came with the place. Just glad they didn't put it over there." He nodded toward the coffee maker. "Then I'd have to look at it all the time." The man handed my husband his credit card. "Storm might come in tonight," he said. "Maybe snow. We can still get hit pretty hard up here even this late in the season." He pushed a key toward us. "Good thing you two aren't in a rush. You look beat."

"Long drive," my husband said. He blinked his eyes nervously.

"Maybe food would help," he said. "Nothing open in town now, but a half a mile out there's a Mexican place—Desperados—might still be open. You'll see a sign on the road."

After we dropped our bags in the room, we got back in the car.

"I'm not really hungry," I said.

"You'll sleep better if you eat something."

Back on 395 we drove out of town and into darkness. My husband switched on the high beams, the road and the thick forest framing it coming to life. We'd driven this stretch many times but always in the morning, after check-out, on the last leg down to the desert, to Death Valley, where the heat rejuvenated us after wet, dreary San Francisco winters.

"Maybe we should have used fake names," I said, on the look-out for the sign.

"Relax. No one knows we're here. What did he say the name of the place was?"

"Desperados. But I don't remember there being anything out here."

"There it is," my husband said, the headlights flashing on a sign at the road's edge, a gun-slinging bandit and an arrow pointing the way. My husband turned, driving down a short, bumpy road nestled in forest, pulling up to a ranch-style restaurant, a large picture window in the front. The light above the door was on and a car, an old Cadillac, in the lot, but the rest of the place looked nearly dark.

"I hope this isn't another wild goose chase. I've had enough of that for a lifetime." A dozen butcher knives stabbed into the deck rails, bullets scattered in between, the vile threats, but because we all lived in the same building, in an HOA, the common space a free-for-all, the police said they couldn't do anything, not until our neighbor actually hurt us.

My husband turned off the engine. "We might as well check it out." He opened the door and got out.

"A Mexican restaurant in the middle of nowhere. Weird," I said.

"Only because it's dark. You wouldn't think so during the day. Everything looks different during the day."

We paused at the door, which was massive, made of thick wood. Carved into it were small gargoyles, human arms wrapped around lion heads. The sign, hanging from a nail, said *Cerrado*.

"See," I said, but my husband pushed on the door anyway, and we stepped in, everything inside—the terracotta tile, the paper lanterns, the wooden booths—giving off a soft reddish haze. From the back of the restaurant a tall, gray-haired man with a mustache appeared. He smiled warmly. "Welcome. We have your food ready." The man slipped back into the darkness.

I looked at my husband.

"Don't say anything," he said.

Then the man came back, handing my husband a white plastic bag. "Enjoy," he said.

My husband pulled out his wallet, but the man raised his hand. "It's on the house."

"Really? Are you sure?" my husband asked.

The man nodded. "It's the end of the day. It's the least we can do. Just come back to see us again. Okay?"

"Thank you," my husband said, taking the bag. "That's generous of you."

The man escorted us back to the front door and held it open for us. Good night," he said.

Behind us we heard the lock turn.

As we headed toward the car, I stopped, turning, and saw the man at the window. He raised his hand, and I raised mine back. Then I caught up with my husband and got in the car. He handed me the bag, and I put it on my lap.

"The guy from the motel probably called it in," my husband said. "He didn't want us to go hungry."

"Whatever it is," I said, "it's still warm."

My husband turned on the lights and then drove out of the lot.

Back at the motel, we lifted the lids off the tins, inside tacos, rice, refried beans covered in cheese. I stared at it for a moment, a long time since I'd had an appetite. My husband unwrapped his fork and plunged it into the beans. Even in the best of times, he was lean, but now no one would guess that beneath his bulky sweater he looked like the starved men of concentration camps. He'd been just as scared as I was. I pushed my tin toward him.

THE DREAM ALWAYS started the same way our trouble had—with exploding glass as loud as a gunshot. Then we'd jumped out of bed and run to the back kitchen door; there, opposite us, was our neighbor's kitchen door, between the two, glass scattered all over the landing, the shards still left in the frame like monster teeth. In my dream though a face—wild-eyed and fiendish—always appeared. That's when I always woke, jolted out of sleep, heart racing, just as we both had been the night it had all started, the night we'd called the police. That's when he'd become vengeful, starting after us, his mania out of control. Tonight was no different, the dream replaying over and over. I switched on the bedside lamp. 5:00 a.m. now, it was still dark, the room chilly. I got out of bed and switched the heat on and then got back in. I didn't see how it would end: months of 5150s at the county asylum, giving us brief reprieves—three days of commitment, two days of post-medication stupor, then the rage would start up again, an endless cycle. The police eventually told us to get a gun. One officer even showed me what to do if he cornered me in the basement or the garage. I looked at my husband now. His face a mask of calmness, he slept so quietly that I felt for his heartbeat, gently placing my hand on his chest, so thin that I could feel the curve of his ribs. Then I got up again and went over to the window and parted the curtains a little. But there was no wind, and now, tucked away in this little room in a mountain town, I suddenly felt safe. I went over to my suitcase and pulled out my jacket. I slipped my feet in sneakers and walked to the back of the room to a sliding glass door and pulled it open. The cold air blasting in almost made me slide it shut, but I stepped out anyway, a long time since I could open a door without fear.

WHEN MY HUSBAND WOKE, I was already dressed. Curtains parted, sun was streaming through.

"Muffins and juice at the front desk if you want," I said. "Sleep well?"

My husband yawned. "Well enough. You eat?"

"I had some tea."

The phone rang.

My husband and I looked at each other.

"You didn't tell anyone, did you? Not even your sister, right?"

"I just told her we were leaving," I said

"Just let it ring," he said.

"He knows we're here." I walked over to the nightstand, picked up the receiver put it to my ear, then pulled it away. "Hang-up."

"That doesn't mean it was him." My husband got out of bed. "Could have been anyone."

"Sure. Anyone." I walked over to the window and looked out, our car the only one in the lot. Then I turned back around. "Did you bring the gun?"

My husband unzipped his suitcase and started rifling through it. He pulled out a map and spread it open on the bed. "Someone will kill him or he'll kill someone, and it won't be us. Listen, I have an idea. The storm's petered out. Let's just take a day off. We're safe. The cats are safe. No one knows we're here. We can take the road into Bodie. It's about twenty miles. It's right here on the map. To that ghost town we always pass. First, though," He went back to his suitcase and started pulling out some clothes. "I'm going to grab a cup of coffee."

IN THE CAR, we got back onto 395.

"By the way," my husband said, "it was the guy at the front desk that called this morning. Called the wrong room."

"Really? Why'd he hang up?"

"Embarrassed, I guess. Worried he'd woken us up. Anyway, he told me to tell you he was sorry."

"Did you have a muffin?" I asked.

"Sure. Chocolate chip. There were tons of them, even though nobody's here."

"What else did he say?" I asked.

"You know, the usual. What you'd expect. Wife left him. Short stint in law school. Hamsters. He's got a whole bunch of them back there where he lives."

"But how could he call the wrong room if we're the only ones here?"

My husband slowed down. "I think that's it—the turn-off." He turned onto an unpaved road.

"You sure? Why isn't it marked?"

"Because it's haunted. The ghosts want to keep it that way. Stop worrying, will you."

The road started climbing through open meadow. Beyond the meadow, on my husband's side, were snow-topped mountains with low-growing sparse vegetation. Out my side a thick line of trees backed a series of bald, rocky hills, but despite the warm sun streaming in, the place felt cold, forgotten.

"What's that ahead?"

My husband slowed down coming to a stop. "Deer. No. Antelope, I think. Two of them."

The pair, poised at the edge of the tree line, were looking down the road toward us. The larger one, the male, I assumed, stepped into the middle of the road, honey-colored, stout, as tall as a horse with black antlers. Nostrils flared, he stamped one foot and snorted. Then there was an explosion, and I fell forward, folding myself in half. "Jesus, what was that?"

"Hunters."

I started to sit back up. "I thought this was a state park."

"Not all of it, I guess. Are you okay?"

"How close do you think that was?" I asked.

"Probably not very," my husband said. "Sound echoes out here. You still want to go?"

"If you think it's safe…"

My husband started driving again.

"What happened to the antelope?"

"I'm sure they're fine. They can run." Having just reached the crest of a hill, he slowed down again, the town coming into view, a bunch of broken-down wooden buildings scattered across a barren hillside. "There won't be any shooting here." He pulled into the lot, a truck there and a cinderblock restroom.

"You think it's flush?" I asked.

We didn't talk much as we walked the dirt and pebble path from one building to another—from the church, the jail, the saloon, to the general store. Mostly we just peeked through windows or barred doorways at what was left of the old furnishings, trying to imagine what life would have been like if the place was teeming with miners, drunks, prostitutes, thieves, children. At the schoolhouse we could see small wooden desks and chairs and old books, readers from the era, and a chalkboard, and there was a spiral staircase up to a second floor. We tried pushing on the door, thinking we might somehow get in, but then I felt a firm hand on my shoulder and swung around.

"Hey, you can't go in there," a red-bearded man in overalls said, a shovel in his hand. "These buildings aren't safe. Half my day's spent propping them up."

THAT NIGHT WE ATE across the street from the motel, at the Bridgeport Bar & Grill, a white-shingle house converted into a downstairs restaurant and an upstairs motel. White scalloped curtains hung over the windows, and on the tables were gas-lit lamps. There were eight tables in total, two against the windows facing 395, four alongside the other two walls, and two in the center where we sat.

"Now what?" I said.

"We order," my husband said.

I closed my menu. "I mean tomorrow."

My husband shrugged.

"Maybe we should call the police," I said. "Maybe they locked him up again."

"The police won't tell you anything. They can't. Not when they're crazy."

"They'd tell us if he were dead."

"He isn't. That's the problem with these guys. You can't ever kill them."

"This morning you said someone would."

My husband opened the menu. "What are you getting?"

"What are we going to do?"

"We're going to wait him out. Something will happen. He'll do something, and they'll put him in jail or in the hospital again and get him right. He can't stay crazy forever. And then we'll go back and start over."

"So you don't think someone will kill him?"

"Do you want someone to kill him?"

"Hey, folks." The waitress stood at our table. "What can I get you?" She pulled out a small pad.

"Coke, please," I said.

"Two," my husband said, and then she went through the specials, venison stew in red wine sauce and rack of lamb with mint butter and mashed potatoes. "Think about it," she said, turning for the bar.

My husband closed his menu. "I say we head down to Death Valley. A week there. Then we go back."

"Why a week?" I said.

"How long can we keep the cats cooped up?"

I rubbed my eyes. "I know. The cats."

"It's only been two nights," my husband said. "Don't worry."

"You don't think he can get to them?"

The waitress placed our drinks on the table and pulled two straws from her apron. "Ready?"

THE NEXT MORNING while my husband loaded up the car, I went over to the front desk and laid the key on the counter.

"So you're leaving," the man said. "Was everything all right?"

"Yes. Fine." I pushed the room key toward him. "About that call yesterday. We were already up, so no worries."

The man raised his eyebrows. He picked up the key and hung it on a hook. "Are you all right?"

"I'm fine."

"You know, you don't have to go if you don't want to," he said. "I can give you a special deal."

"A special deal?"

He took the key off the hook and pushed it back toward me. "For as long as you want."

I peered at the key and then looked up at the man. "What did my husband tell you?"

The man shook his head and shrugged.

I pushed the key back. "We have to go back sometime."

"No, you don't. You could stay here forever. People do."

"But we're the only ones here." I looked down at the key again, its sharp ridges, and then over at the door. "We can't live our lives in a motel."

Chuckling, the man stuffed his hands in his pockets. "Course you can."

Rock, River, Salmon, Sky

The job itself, teaching teenagers on the brink of a downward spiral, wasn't why I accepted an invitation from Oren, the department chair, for a look around. To live at the foot of Mt. Lassen, in the rugged, unpopulated mountains of the Southern Cascades, was. At least that's what I told myself when my husband, David, who'd been invited up too, rattled off the plan: after the interview we'd camp in the park, then hike the summit the next day. The job, according to him, was in the bag—the interview a formality—but the job wasn't like any other I'd had before, and I'd fudged some on my letter and resume, saying I'd worked with troubled teenagers when I hadn't. But then again who wasn't troubled, I rationalized. Still, if Oren pinned me down, I didn't know what I'd do. If nothing else, I'd told myself a few days before the trip, David and I would have a nice weekend away from the city.

But that wasn't to be either. David came down with flu, and by Saturday he was too sick to camp. Half relieved, I planned to cancel, but David, sprawled on the couch ogling wilderness pictures from the Lassen School catalog, said, "What's the worst thing that can happen?" This was what he always said when he'd dragged me down a slippery trail or off a marked one to scramble up some crumbling precipice. So reluctantly I went up alone.

After two hours on I-5, a flat, four-lane highway with few exits, I stopped in Red Bluff, a dusty town of one-story motels and run-down metal diners. At a gas station, I filled the tank and picked up a *Red Bluff Gazette*. HAVE YOU SEEN ME? was the headline, and beneath it a picture of a pony-tailed girl. Upset by a boy who'd turned her down at a school dance, she'd stormed off into the night; all they'd found of her the next day was her shoe at the side of the road. Back in my car, I thought of turning back, deadheading home. Tired and hungry, I craved the familiar—my husband, my urban existence, the malaise of stability—the very things I was fleeing from.

A half hour later when I entered the sun-burnished foothills, where speckled cows mingled pleasantly under shady oaks, I felt better. At least the cows seemed happy. Racing along, the only car on the road, I passed a quaint brick building, the Whitmore Post Office, and a wood shack, the General Store, where I stopped to buy a candy bar and change my clothes and thought life up here might really be as I'd imagined, secluded and simple. David could hike, and I could teach. No one would know us, and we'd know no one. Even the old woman behind the counter who'd eyed my twenty-dollar bill suspiciously reaffirmed that notion: I was a stranger; up here everyone was a stranger. That meant no obligations, no distractions. Hopeful, I turned left onto Lassen-Whitmore Road, which, according to Oren, would climb steeply up to 5,000 feet, where the Mt. Lassen School was located.

Oren wasn't lying. Soon I found myself maneuvering switchbacks, zigzagging my way up a narrow road through a thick forest of trees, which all but blotted out the sun. After several miles the trees opened up some, letting more sky through, but a solid ceiling of cloud had formed, and it was freezing. I turned on the heat, amazed by what swirled from the sky—snow, in June. Why hadn't I checked the weather forecast? The chains, I realized, had never gotten back in the trunk. In such a rush to leave this morning, to get the trip over with, I'd left them in the garage. The switchbacks ending, I was going down a gravel road, and for a moment I thought I'd made a wrong turn, that I was driving down a gully, but then a massive black gate, one side open, came into view. The Mt. Lassen School, woven in wrought iron, arced over the top of it, and as I passed under a broad, flat vista so starkly different from the thickly treed steep switchbacks I'd just climbed opened before me: first, a huge, empty parking lot, then a vast meadow, a rolling patchwork of green, gold, and rust dotted with cabins, and in the distance Mt. Lassen itself, a massive ice-encrusted volcano fronted by a thick wall of forest. Pulling into a spot, I gazed out the windshield, transfixed by the scene. Then I spotted a large man on the meadow moving quickly toward me—Oren, I figured. Stocky with a head of white hair—half cowboy, half teacher—he looked the way he'd sounded on the phone. Before I could get out of the car, he was already reaching in for my hand, but I couldn't tell if he meant to shake it or help me out of the car.

"I'm Oren. We thought you were lost. Where's your husband?"

"Sick. Came down with a flu the night before," I said.

As he led me to a large wooden building, steepled like a church, he told me about the founding families, the Smiths and Allgoods, and then he regurgitated the Lassen philosophy I'd read about in the catalog—stuff about removing troubled children from their environment, about how pitting students against the elements during the required backpacking trips could rebuild confidence. Then, holding the door for me, he said, "The cafeteria's brand new."

"Smells new," I said, inhaling the sweetness of fresh wood, taking in the spread of tables and high, rectangular windows that faced the meadow. In front of one stood a tall, gaunt man in black sweats. The rest of the tables and chairs were empty, the kids gone home for the summer.

"This is Kirk, my fellow teacher," Oren said. "You'll be team-teaching ninth grade English together. *Romeo and Juliet,* isn't it?"

Kirk pulled a chair out for me and smiled, the corners of his small green eyes wrinkling. He wore a black turtleneck shirt and was gray at the temples, though younger than Oren. Something about his slow careful gestures, his pale hands, which he folded on the table, made me think he'd been a surgeon or a pianist. "Where's your husband?"

"Sick," Oren said. "Couldn't make the trip."

"What a pity," Kirk said, "we were looking forward to meeting him. Except for the kids, we don't see many people up here." Kirk took out a piece of paper from his pocket.

Recognizing it, I stiffened, nothing worse than interviewing for a job you weren't really qualified for, the job advertised in a small college newspaper where I lived—just a two-line ad with a P.O. box in Whitmore.

"We noticed from your resume," Kirk said, "that you've worked with troubled children."

"I teach at a school for kids who can't adapt to the traditional curriculum." It sounded lame, but I didn't think what I really did—teach kids who were academic screw-ups—gave me any insight into the battered, the addicted, or suicidal children of the rich that seemed to wind up here.

"Well," Oren clapped his hands together, "I liked your writing." He was referring to a sample they'd requested. He pushed his chair back and stood up.

For a moment I thought the interview was already over, Oren suddenly realizing they'd made a mistake, I wasn't the right person for the job, but he said, "That poem about your father throwing himself from a car, rolling like an egg—that was something." He glanced over his shoulder at the steam rising from the food counter. "Chow time."

At the counter I slid my tray along the metal bars, odd that they'd get the whole kitchen going just for three people. Behind me, Oren fiddled with silverware while a woman in a white uniform heaped a steaming volcano of beef and noodles on my plate. She had the bland face, the pulled-back, colorless hair of those who serve and clean-up. Waiting for my plate, I tried to make conversation. "My high school cafeteria didn't look a thing like this," but all she said was "You're welcome."

Back at the table, waiting for Oren and Kirk, I looked out the window again. It was snowing harder now, the flakes so large I thought I could see their patterns, and on the ground a small gray squirrel, frosted white, zigzagged across the meadow. Then suddenly a dark shadow swooped down, a hawk of some sort, skidding along the snow scooping the squirrel up.

"What we really want for this position," Oren said, placing his tray down beside mine, "is another woman."

Kirk took his place at the opposite side. "The girls need someone they can relate to."

"That's right and the woman you're replacing—I'm sorry." Oren unfolded his napkin. "I know you wanted to meet her…"

"Homesickness," Kirk said, "is a real problem up here."

"She cut out last night. In the middle of the night," Oren said. "Never even said goodbye."

"Well," Kirk said, "she wouldn't be the first."

"And probably not the last." Oren chuckled.

Peering down at my plate, at the volcano concave now in a puddle of gravy, I shivered a little, having left my coat in the car. Suddenly the cafeteria no longer felt cozy but cold.

"Heat's turned off in the summer," Oren said, "even though it seems every summer we get at least one freak storm."

"Do you have some place to stay for the night," Kirk asked, "just in case?"

I looked out the window, the meadow now veiled with snow. Then I slid some noodles in my mouth, thinking I should make an excuse, say I wanted to get my coat, and then drive off. But then again I didn't have any chains, not even snow tires, and Oren, I suspected, would want to escort me back to my car. Maybe the gentleman in him, maybe something else. Turning to Kirk, I said, "So what brought you up here?"

Smiling, Kirk pointed his fork at Oren. "Oren here kidnapped me."

Oren wiped his mouth and nodded. "That's right. From the monastery where he was a monk. You see, I'd heard an ex-professor had been hiding out there, but I couldn't persuade him to leave—that's why I had to kidnap him. So one day I hid behind a tree—one of those great big redwoods—while Kirk was ambling down a path in his robe and sandals and..."

"The truth is," Kirk said, "at first I didn't want to go, but my wife had long since left me. Like you, she's a poet."

Nodding, I smiled, peered into his eyes, two green planets shot deep into their sockets.

"A very good one," Kirk said.

AFTER LUNCH, Oren and Kirk led me across the meadow, continuing their orientation. They described the school's attributes—the Olympic-size pool, a championship soccer team called the Volcanoes. Then Oren told his own story—divorced, with grown children, a refugee of the Redding School District, his favorite novel *Death Comes for the Archbishop*.

Listening, I recalled a picture I'd seen in the school catalog of a much younger, leaner Oren dressed in black pants and a white button-down shirt, reading to a class from an open book, and it occurred to me as I trudged across the snowy meadow between the two men that at some point I'd be expected to tell my story. But what was my story? Mine had started with a lie.

"Now isn't she a sight?" Oren came to a stop and exhaled a cloud of vapor.

I jerked my head up, then realized he was talking about Mt. Lassen, and for a moment we all stood together, peering up at the volcano. Ragged and icy, peak shrouded in cloud, it looked like a fallen planet.

"You're shivering," Kirk said.

"My jacket's in the car," I said.

Oren pulled off his jacket and draped it over my shoulders. "Inside with you then." Oren started marching up ahead toward a cabin.

"Teaching here," Kirk said, "isn't like teaching anywhere else. Here, they let students confront you about your own problems."

I stopped. "What do you mean?"

"They encourage that sort of thing, at forums and such. I went to one once, when I was new like you, and I found myself down on my knees, weeping." He started walking again. "Oren will want you to attend one. You'll have to if you want the job." He climbed the steps and held the door open for me.

Inside was a classroom, three desks pulled together. "Please," Oren gestured.

I took off Oren's coat and slung it around the back of the desk. A little snow slid off it onto the carpet. I touched my hair. It felt damp and cold, and my shoes had turned a deeper shade of beige at the edges, the soles soggy.

"Now you're probably wondering," Oren said, "if we've had any trouble up here, and I want to assure you." He sliced the air with his hand. "Not even a fist fight. Sure, when they first come up, they lie, they steal, but that usually stops after a few weeks, and if it doesn't we put them under abeyance."

"But abeyance usually doesn't last longer than a month," Kirk said.

I looked from Kirk to Oren, still cold, and now thirsty from the heavily salted food. I looked over at the chalkboard—*The great wings beating still / Above the staggering girl, her thighs caressed / By the dark webs.*

"Otherwise," Oren said, "they run away."

"But that's rare," Kirk said, looking at me, then at Oren.

"Well," Oren said, "there's no walls at Lassen. But that doesn't matter. The kids rarely get that far. Usually we find them huddled in the phone booth at Whitmore, at the General Store, shivering."

"Pleading with their parents to take them back," Kirk said.

"Do they?" I asked.

Oren made a tent with his fingers. "The reason these kids are here is because their parents messed up. It's either us or a lock-up facility, and if you have the money it's going to be us." Oren rose from his desk and shook his head. "You won't make it home in this weather. You'll need to stay. I'll phone your husband for you. Kirk will take care of you." He got up and walked out the door.

"My truck's behind the classroom here," Kirk said. "It's much too cold to walk. The way you're dressed." He got up and held the cabin door open for me.

"I'd rather you drive me back to my car," I said as we got in and he started the engine. Between us the gear stick vibrated, and out the window, through the snow, I saw Oren trudging across the meadow, back to the cafeteria, where we had all started.

"It'll be warm in a jiffy," he said, turning the heat on strong. He cut the wheel sharply and drove around the cabin. "You know you can't go home. Soon it'll be white-out conditions."

I looked out my window. Everything was white, and it was snowing harder.

"There's nothing to be afraid of. You'll be put in the consultant's suite." He let out a laugh. "Which is the other half of my cabin. A duplex."

A few minutes later he brought the truck to a stop alongside another cabin, a more weathered version of the cabin we'd just been in, snow piled on its roof. Kirk got out and then came around my side and led me lightly by the elbow up the snowy steps. "Your key's in my room," he said, unlocking one of the doors.

Inside, lamplight illuminated four paneled walls, a cot against one, a wooden dresser against another, and a small desk beside the door. From the ceiling hung a rusty bicycle. "That's better, isn't it?" Kirk pulled open a drawer from the dresser and pulled out a sweater. "It was my wife's, but I think it'll fit you."

I sat down on a chair at the desk and looked up at the window, at the gray-blue light, the storm between the curtains, then back at the sweater again, still in Kirk's hand, a red cardigan with little pearl buttons. "Who are the consultants?" I asked.

Kirk, sitting on his bed, said, "Scouts. They evaluate private schools for parents too busy to do it themselves." Kirk leaned forward, stretching his arm toward her. "Here. Slip on the sweater. Please. You must be freezing."

"Do you have a phone in here?" I asked, taking the sweater and putting it on my lap.

"Back at the office there's one, but I'm sure Oren's already spoken to your husband. You'll be able to cut out tomorrow once they get the roads plowed."

I nodded, looking at the wall behind him, drawings of crumbling walls taped to it, and beneath them poetry written in long hand. *Something there is that doesn't love a wall…*

Kirk looked over his shoulder. "My students did those, 'The Mending Wall.' I teach it every year, but you look tired. There's a bathroom over there."

"I'm fine," I said, but got up anyway, laying the sweater on the chair. Inside, I turned on the water, then splashed some on my face. Red-eyed and pale, I could have been the lifeless woman behind the counter dishing out food. I opened the medicine cabinet, in it a brush, comb, toothbrush, tube of toothpaste half used up, and bottle of aspirin, label worn away. Nothing out of the ordinary. I shut the cabinet, turned off the water, and sat on the lid of the toilet, peering at the door that separated me from Kirk. If there were only a window, I might climb out.

"I want to show you something," Kirk said.

Back in my chair, the sweater on my lap again, he moved toward me, opening a drawer, pulling some papers out. "These are my wife's." He handed them to me.

I peered at the typed poems, unsure what to do.

"She's good, isn't she? Your poems—the ones you sent to Oren—reminded me of hers." He took a few steps backward, then sat on the bed again. "Please, read one."

Afraid to say no, I tried to skim a poem, but my mind was useless; I was cold and afraid, my eye stuck on the title: *Rock, River, Salmon, Sky.* It sounded like a mantra. Like something Indians would say. "I think I'd like to go to my cabin now," I said, standing up, still holding the cardigan.

"Of course," Kirk said. He got back up again and, leaning over me, opened a smaller drawer in the dresser, pulling out a key, and then led me back out. "There's an electric heater on your side. Tomorrow you'll attend an abeyance session. I had to too to get the job. You'll just observe and then you'll be expected to reveal something about yourself. You might need to scream. It's better if you scream."

"What?" I said. "I thought that was just for the students. I thought nobody was here."

"There's always a small group here, including the Founders. Good night." He went back down the steps and over to his side.

In the cabin, a nicer version of Kirk's, a green gingham quilt on the bed, I switched on the desk lamp and turned the heater on. Sitting on the bed, I slipped on the cardigan, trying to think what to do. Then I got up and parted the curtains. Getting dark now, the snow was still coming down heavy. I rubbed my hands together trying to get warm. Then I went back to the desk opening a drawer. Inside were business cards: *Paulette Jones, Educational Specialist. Angela Myers, MFCC. Rita Dagmire, Psychotherapist.* I got up and locked the door and lay down on the bed, the cabin warm now. I let my eyes close. When I woke up, the room had brightened. Between the curtains, the sun streamed in, and when I stood up, I saw a slip of paper under the door. *Breakfast 10:00 am. Abeyance 11:00 am.* I looked at my watch, 9:30 am, and parted the curtains, Kirk's truck still there. From my bag I pulled out a pen and wrote "I can't" on the slip of paper and then took off my shoes and quietly went out and slid the paper under Kirk's door. Then I ran through the snow, across the meadow, the snow so bright it hurt my eyes, toward the cafeteria where I'd left my car. My arms swinging, I realized I still had the cardigan on, but I kept running; my feet sucked into the snow, I lost my shoes and, stumbling, fell forward. After I got up, I couldn't help look behind me, Kirk outside his cabin, waving.

Like Human

It was love at first sight, I'd been told—Jack and Chelsea, a chance encounter in The Palms a year or so ago, two oldsters each out on an early evening walk. After that, they'd met up for short dates, chaperoned by the English woman. There'd even been a few sleepovers during my father's stints in the hospital. His condo shut up, the English woman would come get Jack, and Jack and Chelsea would sleep together at her house. And now there was talk of a permanent living arrangement, a kind of marriage, but the English woman wanted my permission first, and I certainly wasn't going to give Jack away to just anyone, even though my mother had apparently known the English woman, had mentioned her to me once or twice, before she'd died. And, so, I'd flown in. The night I'd arrived, my father, his usual semi-conscious self, was too doped up to keep his eyes open long, only managing a slurred, "How was your flight," before the lids came down. I didn't bother waking him. What for? End stage MS had bedridden him for years, his legs and left hand shot, the right just agile enough to turn the TV remote on and off. His aides fed, bathed, and changed him, transfer from bed to commode no longer possible. That's why I'd nixed the idea of weaning him off the painkillers, an opiate stupor more humane than reality. Jack, though, didn't have that luxury; my mother, the one who loved him, dead a year now.

So my second day in Florida, I set out to find the English woman. The problem was no one knew her name—my mother only mentioned she lived nearby. Which condo she lived in was a mystery, all of them one-story lookalikes. I doubt my father knew either. He couldn't even keep track of the date. When conscious, he often called me by my mother's name. And because I was trying to manage his care long distance, constantly hiring and firing his aides, most of them female, the English woman, I suppose, was just another woman who passed in and out of his house and life.

Standing in front of my father's condo now, I gazed across the street, the aide du jour standing beside me. "One of those, Miss," she said, pointing with one hand and raising the other to her brow, shielding her eyes from the sun. Down my father's driveway I went, though I wasn't exactly sure which one the aide had singled out. When I turned to ask, she'd already gone, the humidity so oppressive, stifling. I could hear all the air conditioners running. No one was out. The back of my neck damp, I knotted my hair into a bun. Then I looked over toward the clubhouse and the pool, thinking someone might be there, might be able to help me find the English woman. But sunbathing there yesterday, I'd gotten an earful about HOA rules, some oldster spotting my Coke can and cigarettes beside my chaise. So I turned back to the row of condos across the street, stucco boxes like my father's if not for the landscaping, lots of palms, of course, and magenta bougainvillea, thick, green lawns—man-made Florida at its best. I stepped onto the sidewalk. A little gray lizard suddenly appeared by my foot and then zipped off. They were everywhere, the critters. I headed down the sidewalk a ways, thinking I should have waited till evening when it was cooler. But after-dinner knocking didn't sound like such a good idea. Anyone under 65 would be suspect, and saying I was so and so's daughter wouldn't help much either as I doubt anyone, except the English woman, knew my father.

Even before MS, he was often reclusive and ill-tempered, a scientist by training, always concocting things, and a gambler, our family vacations at casinos. I wiped my forehead, could feel sweat trickle down my chest. I looked up at the afternoon sky, normally full of gathering thunderheads, but today the sky was ruthless, flat and clear. For months I'd put the trip off. I hated Florida, all the young bodies baking on the beach, the old ones in line at Kroger's. But back where I lived, in California, my dead mother had been at me for months, hovering in the tree at night, scratching at my bedroom window. So I got on the plane.

I turned back to the row of condos, my eye landing on an open garage. Thinking I might get lucky, I crossed the street and walked up the driveway. "Hello! Anyone home?" I called out. Inside was the usual clutter, open boxes here and there and various oldster contraptions—wheelchair, commode, hospital bed, on it a lone torso, one of those armless, legless, headless mannequins with breasts you always see stowed in attics in horror movies. The male version always seemed to end up being resuscitated at CPR trainings. It was weird, the mannequin. I'd worked in retail once, and the storage room was full of them, naked men and women in full rigor all shoved together in a corner. Still, I kept calling out. "Hello? Anyone home?" Then, as I started to leave, I heard a noise, a box shift. A duck appeared, waddling out of the garage, one of those jumbo Muscovy with the shredded-up faces, dark eyes set in a circle of red curdled skin. I'd seen them before, of course, on past trips. Curious, they'd walk right up to you, all pigeon-toed, and, if you squatted down, they'd come in closer, take you in as if you were a thing to be studied, to be pitied. California didn't have this sort of duck, just your ordinary mallard, curious but wary. Squatting down now, I looked my friend square in the eye. I didn't have many. Divorced, I just worked. Weekends I went to the gym, usually ate out alone, never lost weight. I couldn't stand my neighbors.

"Okay, friend," I said, "now surely you must know where the English woman lives."

The duck, raising itself up a bit, suddenly started bobbing up and down, chattering away.

I couldn't help laughing. Taking it as a sign, I stood up and headed to the front door. Right after I knocked, a chorus of yappy barking greeted me from the other side, but no one opened the door. I knocked again and waited, glancing back at my friend, who at the foot of the driveway now, was watching me. Finally, the door opened, and there stood a woman behind a screen door, a small dog on either side, on their hind legs.

"Oh, you're Henry's daughter, aren't you?" the woman said. "They told me, the aide, that you'd be visiting this week." She opened the door a little, gazing past me for a moment. "Poor soul. The way he suffers. Your father." Then she let me in, and both dogs, floppy-eared, long-haired with the round, sad eyes of the breed—whatever it was—jumped up on my legs. Kneeling, I petted both, Jack, the skinny guy, white with large black spots and crusty eyes, and his cinnamon gal, plump and lively.

"Now that's Chelsea," the English woman said, smiling.

"Hello, Chelsea," I said.

"And of course you know Jack." Peering down at him, she shook her head. "You'd never know it, how miserable he used to be. Those aides—most of them don't care a thing for him. Anyway, I suppose you've heard they're in love, my Chelsea and your Jack." Softening, she smiled a little now.

I stood up, getting a better look at the English woman now, her white hair cut page-boy style, shiny as a wig. She also wore heavy make-up—mascara, lipstick, foundation—fighting cancer or just time. We all were.

"You'll have some tea, won't you?" she said. "Then we can talk." Down the hallway she went, through a small living room into a cramped kitchen where she rattled about. The place smelled a little of dog and was very warm, and I wondered why the English woman didn't refrigerate herself the way the rest of Florida did. In the living room now, in front of the couch, I knelt down and petted the dogs again. A few minutes later tea and cake arrived. The English woman sat opposite me and poured.

"Now don't be a shy one," she said. "Help yourself to some cake."

I took a slice and put it on a plate. Then I sipped my tea, feeling a bit European.

The English woman peered down at the dogs, both settled at my feet. "Now I wonder if Jack remembers you."

"Probably thinks I'm my mother."

"Such a lovely person, your mother. Much too young to leave us. And your father, he must be thrilled to see you. Is he doing better? How long has it been—three months—that he's stayed out of the hospital?"

"A little longer, I think. Somehow he always manages to pull through. He's good at that, taking himself to the brink. On a roll." I chuckled, then checked myself. Few people thought illness funny, and most people pitied my father, but before MS all he ever wanted to do, when he wasn't working or gambling, was sleep or bully my mother. It was hard to feel sorry for a man who'd gotten what he'd wanted, but who could say that? Chelsea raised her head, and I reached down to pet it.

The English woman smiled. "Now Chelsea doesn't take to everyone, you know. You've got your mother's touch."

"Her dogs were her legacy," I said, and then laughed again. It sounded so corny. My face suddenly felt warm, and, feeling a little loopy, I began to wonder if there was something in the tea. Or maybe it was just the heat. I felt myself sweating again.

"Are you all right?" the English woman said. "I can turn on the air conditioner."

I looked across the room to a sliding glass door, slightly ajar. A thin curtain, partially drawn back, moved in the hot breeze. "I'm fine. Thank you."

The English woman looked down at Jack. "Poor little guy. He's seen so much illness."

"He's lost everyone he loves," I said.

Jack raised his head a little and then let it sink again between his paws. He closed his eyes. Another hot breeze came through, and I looked over at the door again, to the grass sloping down, the canal somewhere below. "Do you get a lot of ducks out there?" I asked.

The English woman turned her head slightly.

"Now that's where my first baby died, out there, in the canal. Just a baby. Only four years old. She floated up, and I swam out and got her."

Not sure I heard her right, I leaned forward, trying to get a look at the water, but it was too far down.

"You see, I knew there was something wrong when she started acting strange, running in circles, but I couldn't get a diagnosis. They said she was fine. But she kept getting worse and worse. I could see she was suffering. A brain tumor, I was certain. Tumors run in my family. And then one day my nephew was visiting, and by accident he left the sliding door open, and she got out. She was terrified of the water, you know. She would never go near it, so we searched everywhere but there, and then when we couldn't find her and days had passed I was sitting just where you are, gazing out toward the water, wondering if I would ever see her again, the idea came to me that she'd committed suicide, right there in the backyard, and for two more days I sat at the edge of the water day and night—my husband thought I'd lost my mind—and watched and then on the third day I saw her come up, like a star, and there she lay, floating on her belly, her legs all spread out, her long hair, and I swam out there and brought her back."

I put my tea down, a strange feeling coming over me as I sat there, my mind replaying the image—a star rising to the surface.

"My beautiful little girl. White as snow. My Lhasa Sophie." The English woman wiped away a few tears, her mascara running a little. Then she stood up. "Oh, look at me. I'm so sorry. I hadn't meant to talk about this, to keep you so long. And your father—he must be wondering what happened to you."

"I doubt he knows I'm gone."

"I'm sure he does," she said. "He's probably more aware than you think. You'll take some cake for him, won't you?" She went over to the kitchen and brought back a small paper bag. Then she walked me back down the hallway, the dogs scrambling to their feet. At the door I knelt one last time to pet them. "They're getting on, aren't they?" I said.

"Chelsea's thirteen, and Jack's twelve, I think, but they do just fine."

"I didn't know Jack was into older women." I chuckled and stood up.

"You'll be back, won't you?" the English woman asked. "It's been twenty years since my Sophie..."

I saw her tearing up again. "Maybe it was just an accident," I said, though I'd heard of horses doing it—committing suicide. I opened the screen door and stepped outside. Back on the sidewalk, I looked up at the sky. Large, billowy clouds had moved in, the sun shining between them. Still, it didn't seem as hot, or not as hot as the English woman's condo, so I decided to take a short walk before going back to my father's. Heading toward the exit of The Palms, I paused at a grassy area where the residents picked up their mail, peering at the wall of metal boxes, all keyed, a miniature mausoleum, what it always reminded me of. Then, as I started to circle back, I heard a screen door slam, ahead a little boy sprinting across his front lawn. Barefoot, wearing nothing but white shorts, he ran across the street, flailing his arms and screaming, planting himself on the neighbor's lawn, clinging to a palm tree. A woman, following him out, started running after him but then stopped short; looking at me, she shrugged, smiling sheepishly. As I kept walking, passing the boy, he stuck his tongue out and started giggling like a monkey, and it was then that I realized he was older—eight or nine—and he wasn't wearing shorts but a diaper. I rubbed my eyes and kept walking. Back at my father's, I stepped into cool air.

"And how was it?" the aide asked, coming out of the kitchen. "The English woman—did you get her name?"

I followed the aide back into the kitchen. I put the bag on the table. "Cake for my father." She started loading the dishwasher. It was still odd seeing her there, the house always full of strange women with accents, most of the aides Jamaican. "Is he asleep?" I motioned toward my father's room and then went in, over to his bed where the oxygen tank hummed, clear plastic tubing going up his nose, snaking beneath the sheet. As my eyes traveled down his body, from the fleshy arms to the mound of his gut under the sheet, I gasped—the bottom half of the sheet pulled back to his knees, I saw his withered shins, pale white sticks. When had that happened?

"Do you need some help, Miss?" The aide came up behind me.

I pulled the sheet back down and then turned to her, young and pretty, one of the more pleasant ones. Whispering, I started asking her name, but she just laughed. "Don't worry. You can't wake him, you know. Like a dead person he sleeps. Sometimes with eyes open. Like zombie. So did you have a nice visit with the English woman?"

"Yes. Very nice," I said.

"And the dog? Is it okay? Your father said you were worried."

"The dog's fine," I said.

"That's good," she said, walking over to the nightstand and opening pill bottles "to be taken care of."

"I don't understand it." I looked at my father's face. Pale and puffy, it hadn't seen sunlight in years. I went over to the sliding glass door and started to open the blinds, but the aide, turning toward me, said, "Oh, your father doesn't like it. The light and those ducks."

"The Muscovy, you mean?"

"The ugly ones. That's what he calls them. They come to the glass and look in. I shoo them, but they don't go. I don't like them. The way they look at you. Like human." Turning back to the pills, she started dropping them in the pill box, the tiny plastic chambers, closing the lids, snapping them shut.

The Keeper

Announcing the plane's descent, the pilot said the lightning was miles away, but the brilliant synapses lighting the night sky looked close enough to strike. That remote possibility briefly distracted Julia from her fear that someone would find out about the bees. She'd even kept it from her husband, who thought she was visiting her parents because she wanted to. Of course, few visits actually happened that way. For the past twenty years, it was usually an emergency that brought her in, but this trip was supposed to be different, a secret trip she and her father had arranged. That's why the bees were in her tote, in a jar, stowed under her seat now. If her mother found out, she'd put an end to it, might even call the police. The beekeeper she'd bought them from, a man with backyard hives, had shown her how to pull a bee out with tweezers, get it to sting, though she hardly imagined they needed provoking. She'd surely been stung enough as a child.

Midnight, her plane was just touching down now, her plan to take a cab to her parents', not far from the Ft. Lauderdale airport. She figured they'd both be asleep, and then next morning she could greet her mother. Later, when her mother napped, she'd pull the jar out, see if her father still wanted to go through with it. But as she stepped into the empty terminal, she heard someone call her name, a very tall, gaunt man in white shorts. She recognized him right away, even though it had been a long time since she'd seen him, his coarse hair gray now. As he limped toward her, she saw where his leg should have been was a peg and then a prosthetic foot in a white sneaker. Like her parents, Abe, along with his wife Letty, had come south to retire. So her mother had told her.

"I recognized you right away, Julia. You look exactly the same. Like a French doll." Both Abe and her mother were diabetic, and on warm summer nights in New York where she grew up he'd sometimes gather his kids and the neighborhood kids on his front stoop lecturing about the dangers of sugar, of blindness, of limb loss. Now he guided her over to a row of empty seats. "Julia, I have something to tell you," he said.

Sitting against a wall of dark windows, Julia slid the tote between her ankles. In the air-conditioned chill of the airport, it felt warm, the bees beating their wings against the jar. Then she looked over her shoulder at her plane, huge wings barely visible, and out beyond it to the blue-lit runway. "There's a storm out there," she said. "I saw it, on the way in."

Abe chuckled. "In Florida there's always a storm out there." He placed his hand on hers. "It's your father."

She looked down at the tote again, wondering what he'd done, after all she'd gone through. "Is he dead?" What else would bring an old, one-legged man she hadn't seen in nearly thirty years to the airport at midnight? And it wasn't like her father hadn't tried it before.

"Disappeared. This morning. In the car. He took all the pills—the ones your mother hides—and most of the money. Your grandparents are there. They're pretty mad. There's a note too." He handed her an envelope. "It's addressed to you."

She recognized her father's failing hand, her name. But the flap was torn open.

"Your mother. She couldn't wait. You can imagine how upset she was. There was a wad of cash in there too."

Julia pulled out a pink piece of paper. It was folded in half. At the top it said Auntie Pastas, her parents' favorite take-out. At the bottom, beneath the pasta choices, her father had scribbled *I did the best I can. Don't tell your mother. Dad*

They were all lodged there in the living room, her tiny grandmother perched on her father's reclining chair, feet dangling in the air, her mother's dog, a grizzled, half-blind German shepherd, beneath them, then her grandfather standing stiffly behind her like a cardboard cut-out puffing on a cigar. And finally her mother in a white nightgown on the small floral couch, a balled-up tissue to her nose.

Julia put the tote down and then sat on the couch. "How are you, Mom?" She leaned over her to kiss her on the cheek.

Her grandfather pulled his cigar out of his mouth. "Your mother can't talk."

"That crazy dog ate her bridge." Her grandmother, leaning forward, tried to pet the culprit. "Good poochie. Good poochie."

"The bridge," her grandfather said, "is the least of your mother's troubles."

"And your mother's walker," her grandmother said, "for cripes sake it's in the trunk of the car. Your crazy father. How's your mother supposed to get around?"

Julia peered at her grandparents. As a child they'd been her favorites. Family visits to their house in Queens, hours playing on their backyard swing, watching *March of the Wooden Soldiers* while holiday dinner cooked, all the Mountain Dew she wanted, and when she went to college her grandmother knitted her sweaters—and they'd never been mean to her. But lately she'd come to realize they'd had a hand in how her mother was, their philosophy—*make your bed and lie in it*—cruel.

"Julia," her grandfather said, "what are you going to do?"

"Have you called the police, Grandpa?" she asked, though she knew that nobody would.

Her grandfather took his cigar out of his mouth. "We don't have time for that. Your mother's a sick woman. What's she going to do for money?"

Her mother looked up as if she suddenly realized she was being spoken about, mumbling resolutely, "I am not a sick woman." Sniffing, she dabbed her eyes with a tissue. "I can take care of myself."

Her grandfather shook his head. "Your mother doesn't know what she's saying, Julia. What are you going to do?"

Julia sighed. "I don't know, Grandpa." She let her eyes roam the room—the pink walls, white-tile floor, the boys in sailor suits, girls in pinafores, her mother's unfortunate doll collection, their glassy eyes staring back at her. Then she looked down at her tote. *See, I have bees*, she was tempted to say. *Excellent housekeepers, they patch damaged walls, disposing of anything unnecessary, even their dead kin, chucking them out the front door. And yet, they're sensitive creatures. They feel pain.* That's what the beekeeper had told her, a man who took daily stings to his arthritic hands.

Her mother placed her hand on Julia's. "Every time you come it's something."

Julia peered at her mother's hand. It was pale and puffy. Every morning before school, eating her cereal, she had to watch the needle, her mother trying to inject herself in her arm or abdomen, and then during dinner her mother would flick her cigarette ash into her half-eaten food. Capillary blood, tiny vessels growing around her heart, was now the only thing keeping her alive, according to the cardiologist, all the stents, the bypasses, fleeting fixes.

"And now your mother might lose her foot," her grandfather said. "Those sores have to be cleaned."

Julia looked down at her mother's feet, pale and puffy too, one swaddled in gauze. "I thought those had healed up."

The next morning, her mother still in bed, Julia unwrapped the gauze. The wound on her mother's heel, quarter-sized, seemed the most worrisome, a small planet of concentric circles, the calloused perimeter rusty from old betadine, the inner ring, red and scabby, and the center, a circle of milky pink tissue an inch deep. Julia laid a damp washcloth over it, not because she was squeamish—she'd spent too much time in her parents' hospital rooms for that—but because she was afraid any friction might aggravate the wound. That's how she'd come to deal with her parents' crises. She'd moved cross country after college, built a far-away life, only flying in to do what she had to do to keep her parents alive, to keep them from killing each other. And she'd stopped asking her mother to change, to build a life of her own as her mother once had before she'd gotten too ill, working as a secretary to the district manager of Maidenform, a lingerie company. But her grandfather was right—she was too ill now. So was her father.

"It doesn't look too bad," Julia said. She assumed her father had been bathing the foot daily, but maybe it had become too much for him, MS attacking not only his legs but his hands, his left one now limp, useless, a dead fish. Soon he'd have to get a little monkey, she'd tried to joke with him over the phone. She'd read how they could be trained like service dogs, and it made her chuckle to herself, a chattering monkey perched on his chest pushing a straw in his mouth. But her father, doing his own reading, hadn't laughed. He didn't want a monkey—he wanted bees.

Julia took the washcloth off and then with a fresh one started cleaning the smaller wounds, blood blisters on the backs of her mother's toes. Then she started working the wash-cloth up her mother's instep and then down to the soles, to the balls of her feet, all the healthy tissue at risk of infection too. Then Julia looked up at her mother. "Does it hurt?"

Her mother lifted her head off the pillow. "What did he say about me? Does he plan to bring the money back or let me rot here by myself?" Apparently her mother had heard the phone ring earlier. In angry mode now, she seemed to be managing just fine *sans* bridge. Her father too, despite his failing body, had apparently somehow managed to rob the bank account, shuffling stiffly in with his cane, she assumed, since it was gone, making his getaway in the car. Of course he wouldn't tell her where. "Well?" her mother lifted her head again. "Aren't you going to tell me?" But before Julia could answer, the dog came scrambling in, barking, stopping short at the sliding glass door. Its bad eye, cataract ridden, looked like a white marble. "What's she barking at?" her mother asked.

"Ducks. Muscovy," Julia said.

Three large ones were pressing their faces to the glass.

"I hate them," her mother said. "They're hideous. All that red skin hanging off their faces. Shoo them away."

Julia looked back at the ducks again, their shiny dark eyes set in a mask of red curdled skin. "I think they're beautiful in their own way. Curious too. What have you got against them anyway?"

The phone rang.

"Don't move," Julia said. "I still have to wrap your foot." She went into the kitchen.

"I don't know who she is. She isn't the woman I married. She's not. Who is she? Tell me," her father said in a low, harsh rush as he had this morning. Julia looked back at her mother. She was rolling toward the nightstand.

"Is she?" her father asked. "Am I right? Look at her," he said and then hung up before her mother could get to the receiver.

THE NEXT NIGHT Abe and Letty came over. Following Julia into the kitchen, Letty said, "Don't you worry. I know where everything is. I'll pry your mother out of bed." Then, she opened a cabinet and started scooping coffee into a filter. Short and round as a tomato, she looked the same, just grayer. As a small child Julia had spent many afternoons in her kitchen, her mother telling stories over coffee. But the stories weren't always true; well, they started out true, but then her mother made things up. As a teenager it made her furious, her mother sneaking into her bedroom, reading her diary. It wasn't until she was older she understood why her mother did that. Letty nodded to the front door now. "Now scoot. Before it's too late."

Julia cut across the lawn. It was a warm, humid night, the crickets chirping loudly. Turning the key, she pushed the gate open. The small, fenced pool glowed blue. After dropping her towel on a chaise, she stepped into the water and then peered up at the night sky, the moon full, a fat golden globe hanging between two palms, the biggest she'd ever seen, a Florida moon, cratered and scarred. And for a moment she forgot herself, her parents, the bees she carried. With outstretched arms, she split the water, quietly stroking to the other side. Though she wasn't a strong swimmer—had in fact nearly drowned in Abe and Letty's pool as a child—it felt good to move her body after a day of flying and up all night with her mother who, in a fit of hysteria, kept getting out of bed, pulling off the gauze, trying to get down the hallway to the front door.

Now in the center of the pool, Julia turned over on her back, floating. Somewhere a baby was crying; then came a loud splash, maybe a gator dropping into a nearby canal. She turned over on her stomach, peering down to the bottom of the pool. That's where she'd lain, at the bottom of Abe and Letty's pool, on her belly, the blow having stunned her. Once the pain had worn off though, she'd simply rested there and would have stayed had her body not lifted her to the surface.

Julia climbed out, wrapped herself in a towel, and walked over to the fence. On the other side was a road, no cars on it. Last time she'd been here they'd razed a plot of land across the street, one that had been heavily treed, in the branches, birds suspended crucifixion-style—wings outstretched, long thin necks reaching skyward. Now all Julia could see was the faint, round beam of a flashlight, maybe from a security guard watching over the plot.

Back at her mother's house Julia showered and then sat down at the dining room table. The room smelled of coffee. Only her mother and Letty were there now. Her mother, in a floral housecoat and terry slippers, had combed her hair, put on a little lipstick. A steaming cup of coffee sat in front of them. Letty got up and brought the pot in, but Julia waved her hand. "No thank you." She couldn't stand the stuff anymore, the bitterness. When Letty came back in, she started talking. "As I was saying. None of it matters. Money. Jewelry. After I had my surgery I lost interest."

Julia looked at her mother. Stone-faced, she sat staring down into her coffee, lips clenched. "Mom," Julia said, "are you listening?"

"See my scars?" Letty turned her head left and right as if she were showing off a new pair of earrings. A pair of pink parallel lines, short stepless ladders, ran up both sides of her neck, where the carotid arteries ran. Julia had seen such scars before here in the supermarket aisles, Florida full of people cut open.

"The point is," Letty said, "we've been lying to ourselves for a long time. We've abused our bodies. And we have to stop. We have to start taking care of ourselves."

Julia's mother looked up, her eyes teary now, lip quivering. "How am I supposed to live without a husband?"

Letty reached across the table for her mother's hand. "That's just it. It's not easy. You should have seen Abe's stump. It was horrible. I had to dress it. You're a sick woman, and your husband is a sick man."

The phone rang.

"If that's your father, I'm not taking him back," her mother said, suddenly dry-eyed.

Julia went into the kitchen and picked up.

"If you put your mother on, I'm going to hang up. Get me a drink. Get me my pills. Get my insulin. Take the dog out. Let the dog in. I can't take it anymore."

"Dad. The bees," she whispered. "I have them here. If you don't come home soon, they're going to die."

There was a silence. Julia assumed her father had hung up, but then she heard his voice again. "I don't want to fight anymore. I'm so tired. The car's at the airport."

THE NEXT MORNING Julia took a taxi to the airport. At the short-term parking she gazed across rows and rows of cars, realizing it could be several hours if not days, and she might not even find the car. For all she knew he'd made the whole thing up, was out of his mind. But after traversing several rows, she couldn't believe it—she spotted the burgundy Elite parked crooked across two white lines, and to her astonishment she saw through the window all the money in the back on the floor. She lifted the door handle. Not even locked! And fortunately her mother still had a spare key. After stuffing the money into a garbage bag she'd brought, she drove the car back to her mother's, marveling at her luck. Her grandparents would be pleased.

When she got back, her mother was sitting up in bed combing the hair of one of those girl dolls, a rosy-cheeked, blue-eyed one. "This is you," she said.

"I have brown hair, Mom." She studied her mother's face. It was different now, color in it. "You must be feeling better."

"Your father's flying back tomorrow. He's at your aunt's in Chicago. You can go home now."

"Is he? And you're taking him back just like that? Don't you even want to know about the money?"

Her mother stopped combing and sighed. "It's my life, Julia."

"That's the problem, Mom. It's never been your life." She dropped the bag on the bed.

Her mother sat the doll on the nightstand and frowned. "Now why are you so morose? What have we done to you that's so bad?"

Julia walked out of the room. She should have known better. All the times she'd tried getting even, when she'd been in high school, making up diary entries about this or that, a torrid love affair, a possible pregnancy, an older boyfriend she planned to run away with, a high school drop-out, bank robber extraordinaire, the sort of stuff she knew her mother would eat up, but nothing ever came of it. Her mother just kept reading.

Julia went into the garage and got her tote. Then she went out the front door and around back. Kneeling down, she unzipped it and pulled out the jar. The bees, sitting atop a piece of wax paper placed over a layer of honey, were as she left them. The wax paper, the beekeeper had explained, kept them from drowning while the small round hole at the center allowed them to feed on it. Of course, she hadn't told the keeper why she wanted the bees, hadn't told him she'd planned to sting her father, the venom bringing her father's body back to life. Possibly the keeper had already guessed it, had been selling jars to the desperate for a long time. Julia loosened the lid. Then she looked up. The duck trio, back, were waddling across the stiff grass toward her. Then she took the lid off, expecting the bees, finally free, to zoom out. But they just stayed put, so she turned the jar over, shaking it a little, and one finally flew out, landing on her arm. And before she could brush it off, it stung her. Soon a small welt rose and burned, and she had the urge to run inside, crying to her mother as she'd done as a child when her mother, young, untouched by disease, could heal her wound with a Band-Aid and soothing words. But the blinds to her mother's sliding door were closed now. The truth was she'd cleaned up her own scraped knees. And the Muscovy knew it. Gathered around her now, they peered at her with dark, sentient eyes, the flesh of their unfortunate throats quivering as they shifted their round bulk, their ungainly bodies, from one webbed foot to another.

The Prank

"I don't know," Jen finally said, sighing, tired of her father's questions. She really didn't know who was sticking notes and roses under the windshield wiper of her car, and mostly she didn't care—at least she pretended not to.

"Boys." Her father dumped the pieces of his puzzle on the table and began sorting. "Any strange ones been looking at you?"

Jen shrugged. "How am I supposed to know? They're all strange." Leaning forward in her chair, she peered into the mirror, a large octagon mounted on the dining room wall opposite her. She touched her cheek, then her chin. Her fingers slipping down the side of her neck, she could feel her blood softly pulsing. At the hard bone of her clavicle she stopped, ran her finger along the length of it, then looked at her father; he was separating, tossing pieces into piles—a system she'd never understood. Pausing, he picked up an apple, his dessert, and rotated it like a globe, inspecting it for soft spots, dark holes, brown scabs. "Did you wash this off?"

"Anyway," she sighed, "it's not like this guy's an ax murderer or something." She looked at her father again, at his bushy eyebrows, his coarse gray hair growing like Brillo from his scalp. During the day, he wore a white lab coat and wrote formulas for shampoos and hair dyes and thought anything that wasn't washed could kill you.

Her father, shaking his head, bit into the apple and chewed. "You don't know what people will do." He kept chewing, then took another bite.

"Like dye their hair green?" Her father still got calls from frantic women trying to go from black to blonde in one easy step and came out green. *Nice & Easy*—that's what the dye was called.

"We're not talking about hair dye." This time he looked at her from the corner of his eyes. "Are we?" He sat back in his chair and dropped his hands on his lap and sighed. "Look, don't go out alone. When you come home from school, lock the door." He bit into his apple, looked at it as he chewed. "Understand?" He put the apple down.

Watching his mouth work the apple, she imagined his teeth and tongue mashing it up. It was like sitting in front of a dryer, dazed, watching the clothes go round. Finally, detaching herself, she picked up a puzzle piece and held it close to her eyes, as if she were pondering some artifact. But she was really thinking how she'd only run the water—hadn't washed his apple at all, had been running water for the past year, and now some organism might be burrowing its way into her father's mucus membrane.

JEN, WALKING THROUGH the school hallway, counted the black, red, and blue faces, the dials on the locks that hung from each locker—an unending series of miniature clocks silently ticking. "Algebra, the manipulation of numbers and symbols," Mrs. Wolbert had said. "In this class, you're only going to see the tip of the iceberg. In fact, in your whole life you'll probably never see more than this." So then, what difference did it make if Jen was late, if she was thinking about the boy and the sweet nothings he'd been depositing under her windshield wipers in his early morning forays? Last night's note, written in pencil, in his signature sloppy hand, was a repeat of a previous note and apparently the boy's favorite: *I want love with you.* As Jen slipped through the door and quietly wove her way around the desks, all faces turned on her, and her gaze naturally fell on her friend Tammy, a more outgoing, more popular, more troubled version of herself. "Tammy's better half" was what Tammy's mother called Jen.

Mrs. Wolbert, turning from the blackboard, caught Jen just as she was swinging into her desk. "Glad to see you could make it. Having pleasant dreams, were we?" There was a murmur of laughter. Jen felt her face flush.

"Something funny?" Mrs. Wolbert looked from one face to another, as if each face held a secret. Then, she returned to the problem:

$$8y-[3(2y-7) + (y + 1)]$$

Jen copied it into her notebook, but the order of operations seemed arbitrary, like left and right, up and down. As a little girl, the difference had baffled her. Ignoring the problem, she peered at the back of Tammy's head, at the silken curtain of page-boy hair, then over at the tall, skinny, long-haired boy sitting beside her—Tammy's boyfriend Rob. His leather jacket lay on the floor between them like a muddy puddle. At the beginning of each class, he'd shrug it off his shoulders so everyone would have to step over it.

ROB, CIGARETTE in his mouth, pushed himself up onto the hood of Jen's car and surveyed the parking lot of juniors and seniors, all of whom had the privilege of driving to school. "Just look at them," Rob said. He blew smoke out through his nose like a dragon. "It could be any one of them. Aren't you scared?" He looked at Jen, but Jen didn't respond. She knew that he was only half serious, that he was trying to egg her on.

Tammy snatched the rose from Jen, examined its puny red bud, its skinny thornless stem. "Another Seven Eleven cheapo rose." She twirled the stem between her fingers. "Anyone who buys such a wimpy rose isn't worth being afraid of." She walked around the front of the car and eased herself between Rob's legs. "Anyway, it's probably one of your friends, Rob. Or," she smiled up at him, "maybe it's you."

"Or you," Rob said, pushing her back. He hopped off the car, tossed the cigarette on the ground and crushed it with the heel of his boot. Then he opened the back door and got in. "Let's go."

Jen started the car. Tammy, in the passenger seat, flipped the visor down, checked her face, then flipped it back up. "Let's see those notes," she said. Her eyes scanned the front seat, then settled on the glove compartment. She flipped its lid, and there were the white squares of paper. Tammy unfolded one and read it aloud. *I always see you, you not see me.*

Rob leaned forward, between the seats, but Jen grabbed the paper and crumpled it up in her fist. "Do you mind?" she said, as Tammy, giggling, unfolded another. *Who love you? I love you.*

"Who love you?" Rob fell back, laughing. "Poor bastard." He sat forward again and said, "Can't you get a normal boyfriend or something?"

But before she could tell him to drop dead, Tammy, craning her neck around, butted in. "Yeah, like you, Rob, you're every girl's dream." Then, Tammy, turning back toward Jen, started fanning her face with a notebook. "It's so hot. My hair's going to frizz. Can your dad get me some of that no-frizz hairspray? What's it called—*Hair So New*?"

Jen, ignoring them, shifted into reverse. Like her parents, the two of them could get on her nerves, play fight or serious fight—it didn't matter. Why would anyone *want love* with anyone, she thought, as she started to back out?

"Hey!" Rob shouted.

Jen hit the brakes.

Tammy jerked backward, pressing her hand to the dashboard.

"You almost squashed that guy," Rob said. "Are you crazy?"

"What guy?" Jen turned her head.

"Your little lover boy." Rob slapped his leg and laughed. "April Fools."

Tammy twisted back to look at him. "It's not April, and only a fool would wear a jacket on such a hot day. Jesus."

ROB SHRUGGED his jacket off and let it fall on the floor between Tammy's bed and closet. "Plunge," he said, as he fell onto the bed, which extended out to the middle of the room, cutting it in half. Then he leaned over the bed and pulled a joint from his pocket. "A little after school treat." He snickered.

Tammy sat on the floor between the bed and the stereo cabinet and pulled down her phone. Jen sat beside her. There was nowhere else to sit; the bedroom was tiny. The house, a new one, was made up of several boxlike bedrooms.

"Who should we call today?" Tammy dragged the phone book out from under her bed.

"Call home." Rob laughed. He dangled his arm over the side of the bed. Coils of smoke rose in the air.

Jen took a whiff of it, wondering if it would make her high or happy.

"Call yourself," Tammy said, opening the phone book. She pushed it toward Jen. "Pick."

Jen closed her eyes and dropped her finger to the page. "Mabel Murphy."

"Perfect." Tammy lifted the receiver.

Rob sat up, watched himself in the mirror as he sucked his joint. "Perfect," he mimicked, flicking ash on his palm. "When are you girls going to grow up?" He was imitating

Tammy's mother, who more than once had caught them in the act.

"Sounds like an old woman," Jen said, dialing hesitantly. She didn't like pranking old women because they always believed you, even after you started cracking up.

TONIGHT, AFTER she'd gotten home late from Tammy's, Jen stopped in the dining room and turned on the light. The chandelier's tear-shaped bulbs lit the room in soft gold. Her parents were upstairs. She could hear her mother's voice, husky, on the verge of crying, then her father's familiar whine: "What? What do you want from me?" Having to listen to them—to him, his whine more pathetic than sad, made Jen furious, so she only half listened as she picked up her father's puzzle box cover from the table and studied the picture on it: a crumbling castle of bronze-chested men squatting beside small fires, hammering metal. "What world do you live in?" Her mother yelled, had often yelled, though sometimes it was more like pleading, the pathetic gnawing of a trapped animal. Beside one of the men, a woman in a red cloak, hair tumbling down her back in a black waterfall, extended her pale arms to the man. His hammer raised, he gazed into the fire, ignoring her.

Jen laid the cover on the table, then turned off the light. She climbed the steps to the second floor, shut her bedroom door, then turned on the stereo. Lying on her bed, she gazed at the rock stars and actors with tanned chests, tight pants, and white teeth taped to her walls. *If you don't care just let me go*, she sang softly with the stereo. *If you love me say you love me*. She tried to picture his face—his hair, his eyes, his mouth—but she couldn't. She could only imagine a boy, a boy like any other boy, his books tucked under his arm, merging into a hallway of students, a mannequin, hollow, almost human. *Goodbye… Goodbye…*

Jen got up and flicked off the stereo. Wondering why her parents had gone silent, she pressed her ear to the wall. Then there was a knock at her door. On the other side of it was her mother, in her white nightgown, eyes swollen, hair matted down, hovering like a ghost. Dropping her eyes, Jen saw the outline of her mother's breasts, the dark V between her legs.

"I'm going to sleep in the other room," her mother said.

Jen squeezed the doorknob and sighed. "Fine. Why are you telling me?"

"Because your father's a beast."

"Isn't everybody?" Jen felt the sting of her mother's slap, but before she could recover, her mother had walked into the guest room, shut the door, and flicked on the T.V. Between the muffled words, she could hear her mother sobbing, and Jen, pressing her hand to her cheek, ran down the steps, then stopped suddenly at the landing. It was her mother again, this time preserved in her wedding picture. Her mother, swathed in white, the pleated train of her gown spread around her feet like a seashell, looked like her own better half, an ancestor of herself, on the brink of happiness.

A WEEK HAD PASSED since she'd received another note and rose; still, her parents were vigilant, not letting her go out alone at night. In theory, they loved her, Jen supposed. Tonight, though, having licked their wounds, they'd gone out to a movie, leaving her alone with the dog, so right after they'd driven off she unlocked the front door and stepped outside. A humid, sultry night, she imagined herself smoking, vaporous white clouds floating from her mouth. Though she knew where her mother kept her stash, her smoking never went beyond her mind, like most other things. And besides, cigarettes made her retch.

Closing the door, she walked toward her car, which she'd been parking at her parents' insistence beneath the street lamp, and sure enough, she spotted another missive, another rose and note. But this time there was something else, a small silver square. At first she thought it was a square of chocolate, but as she carefully slid it out from the wiper and held it between her fingers she realized it was something else. At the Seven Eleven, she'd seen them hanging on rods, but she'd never touched one before, felt its hard circular rim. Though she should have been panicked—her mother, hysterical, would have called the police—a calmness came over her. She wasn't her mother, after all. Unfolding the note, she recognized the words, a repeat—*I want love with you,* and then she heard a branch snap in the woods that separated her subdivision from another. Peering into those woods, she held her ground, hoping the boy would finally emerge from the dark trees like a bashful deer, but the woods were silent again, and so she unlocked the door, got in, and started the car. Taking the speed bumps fast, she bounced in her seat. She didn't know where she was going. At the stop sign where her subdivision fed onto the main drag, she floored the brake, and the condom and the rose flew off the dashboard and landed in her lap. Slowing down, Jen crossed the main drag, passed a billboard with a two-story shingle house on it—the words *New Family Homes. Superior Living* printed at the top. Then she turned onto an unlit road. As she inched her way down, each skeleton, the beams of a new house, was briefly illuminated by her headlights. Newly developed, the land was flat and treeless as if leveled by a bomb. After pulling up to Tammy's house, one of the first to be finished, she stuffed the rose and note in the glove compartment, then caught sight of Tammy's father in the garage leaning over a ping pong table. She slipped the condom into her back pocket, then got out. Walking up the driveway, she said, "Is Tammy home?"

Tammy's father looked up from what he was doing, sanding the shin of an artificial leg. He wasn't really Tammy's father, though; he was her step-father. Jen didn't even know what to call him. Tammy called him Gary.

"Hey, Jen," he said, "I'm surprised to see you. Tammy told me you weren't allowed out." He kept his hand on the leg as if he were afraid it would roll off the table. At his store he fit amputees and sold wheelchairs and walkers and made enough money to buy Tammy whatever she wanted.

Jen slid her hand into her back pocket where she'd put the condom and shrugged. "I'm all right." As she eyed the tools and open cans, gooey substances dripping over the sides, an image came to her of a legless man she'd once seen sitting on the ground in front of a supermarket. He'd taken off his leg, and it was standing beside him. Jen pulled her hand out of her pocket.

"Well," Tammy's step-father said, "they're inside. Go right on in."

Upstairs she found them squeezed on the bed together, Rob's long feet hanging off. Wearing headphones, he was smoking a joint. He had his eyes shut.

"Hey," Tammy said, sitting up, "what are you doing here?"

Jen walked toward Tammy, eyeing the rose she had in her hand. "Where'd you get that?"

Tammy, plucking petals off the rose, said, "He loves you, he loves me not. He loves me, he loves you not. Rob gave it to me. You're not the only one that gets those Seven Eleven cheapo roses. So how'd you get out?"

Jen looked down at Rob, who still hadn't opened his eyes. He was singing. It was an old song, a creepy one called "Smiling Faces."

Jen pulled the condom out of her back pocket and tossed it to Tammy.

It landed on her lap. "Jesus," she said, recoiling, "what's that?"

"Like you don't know?" Jen put her hands on her hips.

Rob took the joint out of his mouth. His eyelids fluttered.

"Look." Tammy laughed, peering down at him. "He doesn't even know you're here. What an idiot." She put her finger to her mouth, then took the condom and rested it on his forehead. "Get the phone book, will you?" she whispered. "It's under the bed."

"Tammy," she said, sighing. She didn't want to get into another fight with her. They usually had a blow-up once a year. Tammy was her only friend, and what if someone else was pranking her? What if there really was a boy? But she knew there wasn't; there couldn't be, but still the writing—*I want love with you. I see you. Why you not see me?* Why would anyone write that way?

Rob kept singing the words to the song.

"Quick," Tammy said, "get the phone."

Jen shook her head. "What's the big rush?"

Tammy opened the phone book. "Come on, pick."

"You pick."

Closing her eyes, Tammy dropped her finger on the page, then opened her eyes. "Birdie Lyons."

"Birdie Lyons? Who has a name like that?" Jen said.

Tammy pushed the phone forward. "You dial."

Jen, crouching down beside the phone, felt herself slipping back. Still, she said, "I'm not doing old women anymore. I told you. It's mean. If it's an old woman, I'm hanging up."

"Fine," Tammy said, sticking a piece of gum in her mouth. "I have a better idea." She picked up the receiver. "You dial. 6-2-8-7-7."

"Why? What are we doing?"

"2-9. Quick," Tammy hissed, "before he gets up."

"Hello," Tammy said, pinching her nose, "is there a Mrs. Stuart at home?" Tammy snapped her gum. "Your cat, it's on my patio and won't stop meowing. I think it's stuck… Hello?"

Rob, standing, earphones around his neck, held the phone jack in his hand.

"What the hell are you doing pranking my mother?"

Tammy hung up. "What makes you think I was pranking your mother. Maybe you should lay off that stuff. You're starting to hear things." Tammy slid the phone book back under the bed and put the phone on her dresser.

Rob looked at Jen. Then, with the phone wire in hand, he walked toward Tammy.

"Cut it out, Rob," Tammy said, as she inched backward, trapped between her dresser and bed. "That's not funny."

Rob pressed the wire to her throat.

"Rob!" Jen grabbed his arm. "Cut it out, will you?"

Rob dropped the wire and shot a smile back at her. "Just kidding." He picked up his jacket and walked out the door.

Tammy rubbed her throat. "Kidding, my ass."

The door opened. It was Tammy's mother swaddled in a robe, her hair wrapped in a towel. She sat on the bed and looked from Tammy to Jen. "What's going on here? Why was Rob in such a hurry?" She eyed the phone wire on the floor.

"Nothing," Tammy said, plugging the phone back in. "The jack just got kicked out by accident. That's all."

"And you?" Tammy's mother turned toward Jen. "Aren't you supposed to be home?" Her brow wrinkled. "Did you ever find out…?"

But before Jen could say anything, Tammy whined "Mom, why do you always think there's something going on?" She lifted her arms, dropped them, then let out an enormous sigh, as if the world were a lost place. "There's nothing going on here. Is there, Jen?"

A Proper Ballerina

The Ropel house, one of the most expensive in the neighborhood, sat on a cul-de-sac near the woods. Fifteen-year-old Carrie, who lived two doors over, had been babysitting for Mrs. Ropel's six-year-old daughter Simone, as well as other neighborhood families, for about a year. She'd been sitting since she was twelve, first in Connecticut where she'd spent her first fourteen years and now here in Deerhaven, Illinois, where her family had moved last winter when she'd been a freshman, her sister Evie in kindergarten. Though Evie, shy and nervous, didn't make friends easily, Simone and another neighborhood girl, Lisa, befriended her, and much to her mother's relief they all began playing at each other's houses. Meanwhile, Carrie had nearly flunked both Spanish and algebra last year, and she'd not made one friend. But neither her mother nor her father had said a word about this, her mother never one to fret over Carrie: *Drop her in the ocean and she'll find her way back,* Carrie had sometimes overheard her mother say on the phone. And yet, her mother seemed to hold this against her, at times indifferent, if not hostile, toward her; in turn, Carrie often hated her mother, as she did now because she wouldn't admit that yanking her and Evie out of school mid-year for a new house in a fancy neighborhood halfway across the country had been a mistake. If her mother only knew. "Daddy has a lady downstairs. Don't tell Mommy," the Mulvaneys' little Tabitha, tucked in, ready for bed, had suddenly blurted out one night while Carrie had been babysitting. But the basement door was always locked; then one time it wasn't. But she didn't bother telling her mother what was inside. She wouldn't have believed her anyway.

Tonight was the Ropels again, the first time after a two-month hiatus. It all had to do with what had happened to Evie one night, all three of the girls, including Lisa, playing over at Simone's and then somehow ending up in the snowy woods at dusk, an hour later the police with their flashlights finding only two small sets of footprints coming out. "I don't care what the police said," Carrie had told her mother after they'd found Evie. "They left her there. You have to do something. That's not right." And then her mother, finally working up the courage, had said, "I'm going to give that woman a piece of my mind. You're never babysitting there again." But a week later when Carrie had asked what had happened, what Mrs. Ropel had said, her mother slapped her. After that, she and her mother barely spoke, except today when Carrie told her she was sitting for the very nice Mrs. Myers tonight, Mrs. Myers the only neighbor who'd welcomed them on move-in day, leaving a chocolate cake on their doorstep, when in fact it was the Ropel house she was going to sit at. A week before she'd called Mrs. Ropel assuring her all was forgiven. Did she need any babysitting?

At Mrs. Ropel's front door now, Carrie stomped the snow off her boots and then rang the bell. Little Simone opened up. She was wearing a pink leotard, tights, and ballet slippers. With wavy dark hair and milky-brown eyes, a small mole at the corner of her mouth, she was a miniature of her mother.

"Mom, Carrie's here!" She ran back down the hallway.

Carrie stepped inside and unzipped her parka. The foyer was just like in her house, one small closet and a slate tile floor.

Mrs. Ropel was rushing down the steps, as always, running late. "I'm so glad you could make it, Carrie. Here, let me take your coat." In black pants, a billowing blue silk blouse, hoop earrings, she smelled mildly of perfume and was briefly pretty, almost likable, someone she might want to be. But then she thought of her own mother.

Carrie started pulling off her boots, standing them against the wall as Mrs. Ropel hung up her parka. Then, turning to Carrie, she clapped her hands together and bowed slightly. "Well…"

Carrie almost felt bad for her, how awkward it was, despite Carrie's earlier assurances. As is, she wasn't sure she could go through with it, what she had planned for Evie. She looked back at the front door, thinking she should just leave.

"Simone's eating dinner now," Mrs. Ropel said.

Carrie followed her down the hallway.

"Macaroni and cheese." She gestured to the stove. "And there's some there for you too. Simone, Carrie's here."

Simone, at the table, spoon poised above the bowl, said, "I know, Mom."

"Hi, Simone," Carrie said.

Simone looked back and grinned, showing all her teeth.

"I shouldn't be any later than 10:00. Simone in bed by 8:00 please." Leaning over Simone, Mrs. Ropel kissed Simone on the cheek. "Be good. Listen to everything Carrie says. I love you." Then, she went back into the hallway.

Carrie followed.

Back in the foyer, Mrs. Ropel put on her coat and wrapped a scarf around her neck. It had a kind of hood on it, and when she pulled it up over her hair it made her look like a heroine from a tragic novel. "Now be sure to turn the dead-bolt. Don't let anyone in. Everything else is locked." Carrie had heard this lock litany before, which in the past had been merely annoying, but now, after what had happened to Evie, it almost made her laugh. She thought of the Kleins, another family she sat for—they had even more locks—how one time the older boy came at his younger brother with a pair of scissors, Mrs. Klein not believing her, and all those Dr. Spock books on living room shelves.

Mrs. Ropel opened the front door, letting the chill in. Carrie shut the door after her and turned the deadbolt, knowing Mrs. Ropel wouldn't leave until she heard it slide into place. Then, she went into the living room and through the bay window watched Mrs. Ropel's car disappear down the dark, snow-packed road. Now, the place to herself, she could do whatever she wanted, not that she ever drank, smoked, or had friends over. She actually didn't have any unless you counted the two dopey sisters next door that once invited her over to smoke marijuana and put on mascara.

Carrie went back to the kitchen.

Simone pushed her bowl away and wiped her mouth with the back of her hand. "Is my mom gone?"

"Aren't you supposed to use a napkin?"

She slipped off her chair and got up on the balls of her feet, her arms stretched above her head, and started twirling, then fell down on the floor. "I take ballet now. I'm going to be Clara in the *Nutcracker*."

"Doesn't Clara have to spot if she doesn't want to get dizzy?"

Simone got up. "My mom says I get to wear pointe shoes when I'm twelve."

"Is that what you want to be when you grow up—a ballerina?"

"Can I watch TV?"

"Sure. But bowl in the sink first please. Then later we'll play a game."

Carrie went over to the stove and lifted the lid, peering at the gooey orange noodles. Milk, butter, powdered cheese, all the kids loved that boxed stuff, including Evie. She took a spoonful and then stuck the pot in the refrigerator, her eyes roving over the usual stuff—milk, orange juice, wine, chocolate syrup, eggs, chicken breasts, frozen French fries, a Sarah Lee apple pie, and in the door salad dressings, ketchup, mustard, relish, jam. No shrinking heads here, though she'd babysat long enough to know that didn't mean anything, the secret room in the Mulvaney house papered with naked women, and a mannequin in glasses and a wig, two perfect breasts, seated behind a desk. Well, at least her own father used the basement for better things, buying a pinball machine and ping-pong table to ease their move from Connecticut. Evie got a pet hamster too, but it turned out to be pregnant, and she ate some of her babies, so now the table was covered with cages for the survivors, the mother hamster's the most elaborate, exercise wheels and a maze of tubes.

"Carrie, can we make popcorn?" Simone yelled from the living room.

"Sure!" Carrie yelled back. She didn't see any point in not being nice. She pulled some out of a cabinet and stuck it in the microwave watching the bag slowly inflate, and then, after pulling it out, split the bag down the seam, letting the steam out.

Carrie sat down on the couch placing the bowl between them.

Simone, slouched down, dug in, pulling out a handful. "That girl just turned into a blueberry," she said.

Charlie and the Chocolate Factory was on, the petulant Violet in a purple jumper and black Maryjane shoes chomping on a wad of gum Mr. Wonka told her not to touch, the Oompa Loompa men now rolling her out to be juiced. Carrie had seen the movie before.

A commercial came on, and Simone suddenly turned to Carrie, made a pouty face, the corners of her mouth downturned. "Where were you, Carrie?"

"What do you mean?"

"I didn't like my other babysitter."

"How come?"

"She was mean. Mrs. Humperdink. That's a stupid name, isn't it?"

Carrie chuckled. "Is that really her name?"

Simone shrugged and then turned back to the TV, the spoiled Veruca Salt, another bad egg, getting sucked up a garbage chute and then Mike Teavee, shrunk small enough to fit into a TV, had now been eliminated too. Only Charlie and his grandfather left, Mr. Wonka's face softened as he started explaining how he'd searched the world over for just one sweet, able child to take over the factory.

"Can we watch another movie, Carrie?"

"It's not over yet though."

"I don't like this part. It's stupid." Wonka was now escorting Charlie onto his magic elevator. Soon all of Charlie's family would be rescued from poverty. Simone changed the channel, a bald, muscular man, with bushy white eyebrows on now. Grime-busting Mr. Clean.

"Well then maybe we can play a game," Carrie said. "Remember how we used to?"

Simone shrugged again. "Can we watch another movie?"

"I'm *it*."

Thinking, Simone rolled her head around in circle—one of her odd quirks—and then slipped off the couch. "Count slowly. No peeking."

Eyes covered, Carrie started counting "1, 2, 3, 4," stopping only when she heard Simone heading upstairs. She always hid in the same spot. It seemed odd at first, but Carrie had just assumed that getting caught was probably the best part of the game for Simone. And in the past, they'd had fun, Carrie in Mrs. Ropel's bedroom closet pretending to be stumped, Simone, impatient, eventually jumping out, shouting, "Boo!" But after Evie had disappeared, she wondered about those quirks, all those kid things. Simone, sneaking out of the house, past her watchful mother, Lisa and Evie in tow, out into the woods at night took stealth.

Carrie pulled her hands away from her eyes and headed upstairs. In her socks, she could move silently. She took her time, though, roaming around the other bedrooms—first Simone's, cozy pink with a strand of blue lights lining the ceiling, and her very own bathroom with a polka-dotted shower curtain, a furry pink bathmat beside the tub. The other bedroom, blue and smaller, hadn't changed—wooden crib, rocking chair, a three-drawer dresser with a changing table on top. Carrie pulled each drawer open—all still empty. Then, she headed toward Mrs. Ropel's bedroom. A small lamp on the bedstand threw off a little light, beside it a magazine—*Good Housekeeping*—and an alarm clock. The other bedstand was bare, the Ropels separated, Carrie's mother had told her. All the other sitting jobs, the husband usually drove her home in their dark cars, small-talking her, pulling up to her house, as if they were dropping her off from a date. At school the driver's ed instructor kept sliding his arm around her shoulders showing her how the dashboard worked. In the Ropel house, she'd always felt safe though.

She walked over to the closet. It was open a crack. She thought she could hear Simone breathing. It wasn't too late. She could just play the game as they always had. But then Carrie remembered the snow swirling down from the black sky, her feet so cold they burned as she shivered at the edge of the woods while the police searched for Evie, her hysterical mother, waiting at home in her sunken living room, her father trying to comfort her.

Carrie opened the closet door and leaned in. "Hello? Anyone in there?" Then she went all the way in. "Anyone here?" Simone, she knew, could only contain herself for so long, but Carrie continued to play along, turning to the right side first, making a fuss of pushing clothes this way and that way, making the hangers jangle. Then she turned to the other side, where there were a lot more clothes, dresses and blouses, and did the same thing, Simone, she assumed, crouched somewhere beneath, watching Carrie's legs, trying to stay quiet. "Simone? Are you in here?" Carrie let out a loud sigh. "Wherever could she be? Well, I guess she's not here." Then, as she stepped out and started closing the door, the hangers suddenly jangled. But Carrie already had the door shut, her hand firmly around the knob as she felt Simone trying to turn it.

"Carrie," Simone said, "the door's stuck."

Carrie thought she could hear a twinge of fear rise up in her voice.

Simone started banging on the door.

Letting go of the knob, Carrie quickly swung around, pressing her back against the door.

Then Simone started kicking. "Let me out! Let me out! Let me out!"

Carrie could feel the door shuddering, and she pushed back harder on it.

Then the kicking stopped. "Carrie, please," Simone pleaded, "it's dark in here." She started weeping. "Carrie, I'm scared. Please, let me out. Please, Carrie." She was trying the knob again, pulling on it, rattling it.

Was she really scared or just faking? Carrie looked up at the ceiling, at the small ring of light from the lamp. Evie had been found curled up at the base of a tree, unconscious, her shoes missing. After laying her on the stretcher, the paramedics had cocooned her in blankets as the snow kept falling.

The rattling stopped. "If you let me out, I promise I won't tell on you." No longer crying, Simone was trying to modulate her voice now, to reason with Carrie. *Negotiation* it was called, what a victim does trying to survive an attack, something she'd learned in psychology class. But Evie probably didn't even get that chance, Simone and Lisa running off while she was *it*, Evie with her eyes covered, counting, afterward the police claiming it was a game of Hide and Seek gone awry.

Simone started beating her fists on the door again. "That's not fair. Let me out! Let me out!"

So now you know. Maybe you'll think twice. She'd planned on saying things like that, but now Simone was throwing her body into the door, putting all her weight into it, and Carrie, worried she might damage the door or hurt herself, stepped away, and Simone suddenly flew out, landing on her knees. "Oow." She started crying again, real tears now, her lower lip trembling. She glared up at Carrie. "I'm going to tell my mom. You're going to get in trouble." She was breathing heavily, almost gasping. Then she started coughing.

Carrie reached down and pulled Simone to her feet.

Simone wiped away her tears. "I'm going to tell on you. That you tried to kill me. Then you're going to get in trouble. You're going to go to jail. Rats are going to eat you. Then they'll put you in the electric chair, and your hair will fall out."

Carrie stepped back and sat down on the bed. "Who's going to believe you?"

"My mom will. She always does."

"But there's not a thing wrong with you. I bet you don't even have a bruise or a cut."

Simone put her hands out in front of her and spread her fingers. Her knuckles were red, her hands shaking a little.

"See? Not a thing."

Simone pulled her hands back and started rolling her head around again; this time, though, with her flushed face, watery eyes, snotty nose, she looked ghoulish. Then, after wiping her nose, sniffling a little, she straightened up, lifting her chin, like a proper ballerina, and said, "I'm going to get in my pajamas. It's almost my bedtime."

"Do you want me to read you a story?" Carrie was still sitting on the bed.

"I'm too old for that. Besides I'm going to tell on you. You're never coming back." Then she scampered out of the room.

THE NEXT DAY Carrie slept late. She always did on the weekends. Then in the afternoon she went down to the basement to feed the hamsters; the babies, now plump and furry, were running around their cages. The mother hamster, though, just sat in her bedding, her dark eyes unblinking, food untouched. Tapping on the plastic walls, Carrie tried to coax her to move. Then, opening the cage, she reached in to pick her up, but she just nipped at her hand.

"Carrie, are you down there?" Her mother was coming down the steps with laundry. In front of the washer now she put the basket down and then looked over at the ping-pong table. "When it gets warm," her mother said, "I'm going to let her go."

Her mother's eyes looked puffy, like she'd been crying. She was trying to make up, be friends now. But Carrie, still angry, wasn't so sure she wanted to relent.

"If you must know," her mother said, "her baby—Mrs. Ropel's—was still-born. A little boy. She had to carry it and then give birth to it and then bury it. All before we moved here."

"That doesn't excuse it," Carrie said. "Evie could have frozen to death. And then what?" Carrie looked down at the mother hamster and then over at her mother. "What do you mean let her go?"

"Behind the house. Out by the woods. I'll just open the cage."

"But what if she doesn't go? What if she gets eaten? They're wild animals out there, you know." She hammered at her mother.

"What's the point of keeping her? You can't touch her. She won't eat. They don't live very long anyway. Hamsters." Her mother turned to the machine and started stuffing the laundry in.

"Where's Evie?"

"Upstairs. Playing. You know, making her Barbies talk. By the way, I found your bathing suit. I'm washing it now." Her mother shut the machine door and turned the dial. At her old school they didn't even have a pool, but here in Deerhaven there was an Olympic size indoor one.

"Don't bother," Carrie said. "The school won't let me wear it. You have to wear one of theirs." She recalled last Friday, the first day of swimming, naked and shivering, how she stood in the locker room, the attendant sizing her up.

A Pretty Picture

This weekend they planned to see the Julia Morgan again—an exquisite, two-story stucco with soaring ceilings, rich mahogany floors, and lovely built-ins. $2.5 million. Not that she and Conrad planned to buy. On Sundays they just liked going to the open houses, touring the old Berkeley homes in the fancy neighborhoods they couldn't afford. And it wasn't that they were poor. The 1918 condo they'd bought two decades ago was actually quite valuable but not valuable enough to buy one of the grand old houses—there simply wasn't enough cash to make up the difference. Conrad, an accountant for a small business stamp company, did okay, but because he was on in years his meager increases barely made up for inflation, and Dorothy, a therapist with her own practice, was on the downslide too, the scream therapy she gave, corrupted, commandeered now by marketers looking to make a buck. "Log onto *Escape to Australia* and with the touch of a button you can scream your head off, record it, and hear it played back to you from the Outback." Dorothy had stumbled onto the website one day and was horrified to see a giant speaker blaring someone's screams among startled kangaroos. But on Sundays, roaming through all the open houses, she and Conrad could forget their problems. This Sunday though, Conrad woke up with a cold. "But don't let that stop you from seeing the house again," he said to Dorothy after he blew his nose.

"I think I'll go meet Margret instead. For brunch. She's been trying to get me into the city for ages. I'll just take the train in." Earlier, before Conrad had woken up, Dorothy had spotted in the newspaper just a small ad about an exhibit at the San Francisco Art Museum, a new gallery across the bay, beneath it a small photo of a diapered infant propped up on a pillow. But precious as it was, there was something odd about it, the infant's eyes. Dorothy had to get a magnifying glass to get a better look.

"But what about the Julia Morgan?" Conrad asked. "It might not be open again next weekend."

"Oh, they'll be others. And besides I wasn't keen on the bedrooms. All that dark wood paneling. And that pink bathroom. I couldn't see myself squeezing into it. Though that old tile has its charm."

"Well, that bathroom would have to be gutted," Conrad said.

Gutting such houses—the Julia Morgans, the Bernard Maybecks, the John Hudson Thomases—was something they'd become fond of doing, tearing them down to size with this or that comment.

Dorothy slipped on her coat and picked up her bag. "I'm not sure when I'll be back. Before dinner. Maybe we should bring something in—if you feel like eating, that is."

"I always feel like eating."

She left the condo and walked to the station, catching a westbound train. Twenty minutes later, emerging from the tube under the bay, Dorothy got off at Powell Street. It was quiet there, the underground station dingy, only a man in a blue jumpsuit pushing a yellow bucket, a string mop protruding from it. As she rode the escalator up and heard a train from the eastbound side pull in, a pang of regret, of guilt, struck her, and she thought of aborting, of running back down the escalator and catching that train back to Berkeley, where she could leisurely breakfast at a café and then hit the Julia Morgan. Conrad wouldn't know any different, would probably be pleased that she'd changed her mind. After returning home, she could deliver her impressions, and once again together they could tear down the house. Had she been truthful, had she told him where she was really going, the nature of the exhibit, she knew what'd he say: *Why on earth see a thing like that?* But she couldn't be the only one going, could she?

Exiting the station, she stepped out onto Market Street. A heavy dome of fog hung over the city. Shivering, Dorothy pulled her coat tight as she headed toward the museum, along the quiet sidewalks as the empty Sunday buses and cable cars ground down the street.

Outside the museum now, an older brick building that hadn't yet been torn down, she paid and then entered, brochure in hand. For a few minutes she skimmed through the brochure and then followed the signs to the exhibit. At first it looked like any other gallery with framed art hung on austere white walls and benches to sit, though these were polished marble, long and rectangular, attractive but hardly inviting. It was early, only a few people milling about, their coats still on as if the fog had crept in with them. Maybe the photographs, like delicate fruit or the dead themselves, needed to be kept at a certain temperature.

One by one she took each photograph in, mostly families—mothers and infants, siblings, whole families, what you might think were innocent depictions of a bygone era, if you didn't know any better. So it was like a strange guessing game, trying to distinguish the dead from the living. That apparently was the point of such death photography—daguerreotype—developed in the early 1800s as a means to help the Victorians cope with early death, so the brochure said. Print-maker Louis Daguerre had apparently invented the means to make such photos both blurry and lifelike, a loving means of preserving the dead. One photograph in particular drew Dorothy in—five plump, dour-faced siblings lined up in a row, three boys and two girls, the older girl, a sturdy brunette with long, curly hair, wearing a plaid jumper, and the other, the smallest, a cutie with blonde sausage curls, in a white satin dress. Dorothy stepped closer, zeroing in on her. She was a little paler than the rest, her cheeks puffed out as if she were holding her breath, her shoulders so bunched up she seemed perfectly neckless. Her eyes barely open, she appeared to be asleep on her feet, whereas her siblings, erect and round-eyed, seemed unable to shut their eyes, their lids seemingly propped open.

"It's her." Dorothy heard a voice behind her. "The dead one." She turned and saw a young man sitting on one of the marble benches. He had straight dark hair and bangs and pimply skin. He was wearing gray sweatpants and what looked like brand-new white sneakers. He was quite small, the size of a boy, his feet barely reaching the floor, but his deep voice made her think he might be older, high school, maybe even college. She'd treated young people before. She actually preferred them over adults. Dorothy looked at the photograph again and then down at her brochure, which said the smallest bodies were the easiest to prop up. She sat down beside the young man. He was clutching an old, battered-looking shopping bag on his lap. This struck her as odd, but she shifted her gaze to another photo to the right of the siblings. "I thought this might be interesting, but actually it's quite ghastly" came out of her mouth, though she'd meant to keep this to herself. But then wasn't that how she used to always start her sessions so many years ago, before scream therapy, when she'd endorsed traditional talk-therapy, with an icebreaker, a confession of her own? Of course, some of those confessions were just lies.

"The ones with the eyes are the worst," the young man said. "The painted-on ones."

She assumed he was referring to the 19th-century artists who made their living painting eyes on the dead. There'd been something about that in the brochure too, and now that odd picture of the infant in the newspaper made sense.

"Are you a student?" Dorothy asked.

The young man relaxed his grip on the shopping bag a little. "Not really. I was shipped here from China. My parents like to send me places."

"To study? Your English is very good." Dorothy thought it was best to compliment him. It was almost impossible not to when presented with someone this young and obviously ailing. Still, she was surprised at how readily he'd engaged her. She wouldn't ask him about the shopping bag, of course. Not right now.

"When I was in high school, they sent me to boarding school in China."

"Why is that?"

The young man shrugged. "My parents don't get along. They hate me."

Dorothy nodded. She heard such proclamations before, but she'd never met a parent who hated their child. She didn't think it was impossible though. "You seem like a nice person to me," Dorothy said, still peering at the photograph next to the siblings, this one a sweet family trio arranged lovingly in a coffin, husband and wife, their infant nestled between them. Eyes closed. A serene look on their faces. Such a pretty picture.

The young man let out a sigh. A little bead of saliva formed at the crack of his mouth. "Those little beasts at the boarding school tormented me for years."

"That's terrible. What did they do to you?"

The young man turned toward her. His eyes looked glassy. His head shuddered a little, and then, clutching the bag more tightly, he turned away. "Never mind. It doesn't matter."

"Doesn't it?"

"What do you think they did to me?" His voice was almost a whisper now, a polite hiss, which made her bristle. She thought about getting up, leaving. She looked for a window.

But then he sighed. "It doesn't matter. Let bygones be bygones." He chuckled a little.

The expression sounded strange coming out of his mouth. Dorothy folded her hands on her lap, trying to appear relaxed, and looked at a different photo now, this one to the left of the siblings. In it another little girl, this one seated on an uphol-stered chair, appeared to have dozed off, her head turned, chin resting on her chest. Beside her, in a twin chair, was a large doll nearly the same size as her, wearing the same hair ribbon, the same jumper.

"That's definitely the weirdest one," the young man said. "Dolls are so creepy."

"You know," Dorothy said, "I'm a therapist. I can help you."

He turned toward her again. "You came to see dead chil-dren and you want to help me?"

"I don't blame you for being angry," Dorothy said.

"You don't even know me," the young man said.

"What is it you have in that bag?"

He blinked his eyes and then gazed into the bag. "It's what I carry with me all the time," he said.

"You aren't homeless, are you?"

The young man scoffed. "You think everyone who carries a bag is homeless?"

"Of course not," Dorothy said. "It's just that I'm worried about you, that you might hurt yourself. You wouldn't do that, would you?"

"You mean hurt someone else." He looked around the room. "There aren't even enough people here to hurt. I should have gone someplace else."

Dorothy rubbed her hands together, the bench beneath her so cold.

"Anyway," the young man said, "haven't you seen enough? Maybe you should leave. You must have better places to be."

Dorothy imagined Conrad in his armchair, tissues and cough drops, the smell of mentholyptus. She thought of all the bad colds she'd had, how she couldn't breathe. "Actually I don't."

"You're just saying that," the young man said. His face stony now, he reached into his bag.

"You don't need to do that," Dorothy said.

The young man pulled his hand out, in it a thin, dog-eared book.

"Oh," she said, relieved, then annoyed, recognizing that miserable little book. The proverbial bible of alienation—*The Stranger*. How many young men had it ruined? Still, Dorothy remained composed. No point in being argumentative. "Are you reading that for school?"

"Who said I was going to school?"

"I just assumed…" She noticed that there were more people about now, and a few had turned to look at them.

The young man slipped the book back in the shopping bag; then he pulled something else out and stood it on his lap, holding it firmly between his hands. It was so bizarre she didn't know what to say as she stared at its button eyes and stitched-on mouth. Then he put the small stuffed bear back in his bag.

"Is that all you have in your bag?" Dorothy asked.

Another bear came out, this one green with some bald spots around the ears. "This bear hates everyone."

"Why?"

The young man slowly shook his head. "It just does."

Dorothy crossed her arms, hugging herself. "I wish they'd turn some heat on. I've never been so cold in my life."

The green bear disappeared back in the bag.

The young man turned to her. "You'd better leave now."

"Why? What are you going to do?"

"What do you care anyway?"

"Just think of your future." Dorothy wanted to reach out to the young man, to touch his arm.

"You like to play games, don't you?" The young man looked over at a photo. "You know why she did it? The mother."

Dorothy followed his gaze. He seemed to be focused on the family in the coffin. "Did what?"

"Stabbed them with a knife. Him, then the baby."

Dorothy studied the pretty face of the young woman, of the murderess, and then looked down at the brochure. "Is that what it says? How awful." She shook her head. Feeling sick, she pressed her hand to her stomach, and muttered, "I should have gone to the open house, the Julia Morgan."

"Julia Morgan? Who's that?" The young man slid his hand back in the shopping bag, something small and dark coming out this time.

But Dorothy, trying to calm herself, averted her eyes, fixing them on the space, the white wall between photographs. *A tranquil luxury; a quiet grandeur.* The realtor's voice from last Sunday echoed in her head and then the brochure copy, what she could remember of it, she started reciting—"Classic wainscotting. French doors. Curved staircases. Leaded glass. Expansive gardens. Gourmet kitchen. Heart-stopping views. An absolute gem…" She kept it up for as long as she could.

El Diablo

Living at the base of the Oakland hills for many years, I knew the way up well. It was a spring day, sunny, with a cool breeze, a year into the pandemic. I was wearing a light-weight jacket and sweats. Immunized now, I no longer needed to shut myself away, so I started taking my walks again up into the hills, as I'd always done before the pandemic. This way I could pretend my husband hadn't died quarantined in a hospital, that there'd be someone to come home to. It took me a long time to bury him, the undertakers backed up.

Cutting through the parking lot of a hotel near my home, the Claremont Hotel, a ghostly, turn-of-the-century, castle-like structure, I started up the old stone steps, a short-cut up to Alvarado Road, the main drag up through the hills. Then, after crossing the street and walking another twenty feet or so, I mounted another staircase—the Eucalyptus Path—these steps, cement, better maintained, but much steeper and longer, airy houses overlooking the Bay on either side. As I huffed and puffed up, I imagined myself the mistress of one, wandering from room to room in a white nightgown, windows flung open, bay breeze fluttering the curtains. Not that my apartment in the flats was bad. In fact, it was quite lovely, 1920s stucco, with tall windows and fir floors, but it was small and even with my husband gone it still seemed cluttered. In my pajamas I was always bumping into things.

Halfway up the steps now, I was sweating a little. No matter how many times I'd run them, it never got easier. Never enough air. Resting for a moment, I peered to my right where the Sunset Path began, this one flat, ending at another hidden stairway up. The East Bay hills were full of these cut-throughs, these secret walkways.

After continuing up the last half of the staircase, I stopped at the top to catch my breath again. Then, turning left, I headed up Alvarado Street, climbing higher into the hills. No sidewalks, I kept to the road's edge passing more large homes, some Mediterraneans, white-washed, accented with colorful mosaic tile. Rounding a bend, I continued up, ahead two enormous eucalyptus trees, the only ones left, lone survivors of a firestorm that had swept through here twenty years ago. Most everything beyond them had burned.

Standing between the trees now, I peered at a narrow dirt path zigzagging down through reforested canyon into the flats, the only off-road hike up here. On hot summer days I often paused here at its shady entrance, oaks and buckeyes framing the trail, ferns and trillium growing at their base. But no matter how hot it got, I'd always stuck to the road, my husband worried I'd get jumped by a mountain lion. They were all over California, not just in remote places like Death Valley or Anza Borrego but in suburbia along paved trails and athletic fields. We'd stumbled on the remains of their kills a few times. No blood. No fur. Always just a single deer hoof.

I kept walking, the houses here more numerous, these the newer, rebuilt ones with double garages and fire-resistant roofs, the fire incinerating just about everything here and above. Back then it was the dry Diablo winds sweeping down, parching the landscape, sucking out all the humidity, turning a minor grass fire into an inferno that left only charred stumps and masonry rising up from a smoldering wasteland. After the road had reopened, my husband and I had driven up into the eerie scene.

Now though, no one would know that fire had ravaged this place, everything abloom, the birds twittering. Pausing, I turned, taking in the ethereal view behind me, in the distance the placid, blue-gray bay, wisps of fog floating over it, and the Golden Gate Bridge hanging in the air.

I started climbing again. The road not especially wide, rickety gardeners' trucks parked on either side, I kept an eye out for oncoming cars as I admired the lovely spring gardens—the feathery breath of heaven, the star-leafed maples, the orange holly, the magenta bougainvillea massed on trellises—all of it so pretty.

I stopped again, this time in front of an empty lot at the edge of the canyon, one of the few still left after the fire. A house on stilts was being built. No solid walls yet, men were inside the structure hammering. For the people who hadn't made it out, who'd died, the fire spreading so quickly, a memorial garden had been built, down at the base of the hills, near the highway, with a small seating area, poppies, nasturtiums, and other wildflowers blooming there every spring, and plaques with the names of the dead engraved. Back then my husband and I had seen the flames as we stood among the crowd gathered in the Claremont Hotel parking lot, the fire department drawing its line right behind the hotel where a palm grove was burning, their heads alight, and we watched the people who lived there, the ones who'd escaped, watch their homes burn.

Now, though, everything was perfect. Though the road was getting steeper and I was sweating more, I kept my jacket on, zipped up. I knew once I reached the top and started circling down, the road would be shadier, the breeze colder. Coming down toward me now were a few older, white-haired women I'd seen before walking their little dogs, poodles and bichons with rhinestone collars. "Hello."

"Good afternoon," they all said, still wearing their masks, even though they were no longer required outdoors. But soon enough after they'd passed and I'd gotten higher up, near the top, there was nobody, only a few houses pushed back from the road, perched atop a slope. This part of the hills was more remote, more isolated—at least it always seemed that way. But then as I rounded a bend and mounted the last steep hill up, I spotted two gardeners above me, one going at hedges with large shears, the other raking. Then, after passing them, my eye caught something dark at the very top of the hill, at the road's edge.

At first I thought it was a just a shadow of something, the overhang of a tree. Still not used to being alone, I hadn't been sleeping well. Sometimes, thinking I'd heard things, I'd peer down the foot of my bed, expecting to see a shadow—sometimes a man, sometimes an animal. A newspaper article I'd read once described a woman who left her front door open one night only to find a lion crouched at the foot of her bed. But now the shadow at the hilltop moved, took a step or two. It had legs, a dog maybe, some sort of dark shepherd, but I'd never seen a loose dog up here, not this size, this mangy looking, almost emaciated. But then I realized, as it lifted its head, seeming to leer at me, it couldn't be a dog. I stood still, thinking now that it had spotted me, it would take off, disappearing into the canyon, but instead, it started meandering down toward me, dipping its head, wagging it a little, as if it were being bashful or sly. It was also listing sideways as it moved, almost staggering, but then righting itself. I kept my eye on the animal. Its dark face grayed around the muzzle, haunches bony, tail tucked between its legs, it was likely injured. But injured animals didn't come out in the open, did they? There was something else odd about it; its ears, neither erect nor pointed but large and round, were like those of an African dog. I felt my skin prickle, and as

I started to back up the animal lifted its snout seeming to sniff the air.

"What is that?" One of the gardeners, who must have spotted the animal too, had come down beside me. He held his rake upright, the prongs pointing skyward.

I shook my head and shrugged.

"Looks sick. *Muy enfermo*," the man said.

"There's definitely something wrong with it."

He looked over his shoulder down the road. "You better go back where you came from."

The animal, halfway down now, had stopped at the side of the road.

"See? It's watching you, pretending not to see you," he said.

I looked at the animal again, its face slack, vacant now. It looked blind.

"*El diablo*," the man said.

I turned to him. Heavyset, he wasn't much taller than me. "The devil? Out in the open? I doubt it."

"It could kill you. Look at its teeth. If you get bit, you could die. You could go blind and growl like an animal."

Was he trying to scare me? But then again if the animal was rabid, he might be right. I'd heard strange things could happen to people with rabies. "We should get help," I said.

But the man was already backing up.

I turned back around, the animal coming down the road again, its ribcage sliding beneath its skin. I rubbed my eyes, wondering if I were dreaming.

"You better get out of the way." The man was above me now, at the edge of the garden. "It's coming right at you."

I turned back to the animal, but it was drifting the other way now, to the center of the road, its head bobbing, tongue hanging out. *El diablo*—or maybe just some poor animal, lost, half out of its mind. I took off my jacket and wrapped it around my waist and then started to follow. But I was careful, staying on the other side of the road. I pulled out my phone, calling the police who patched me through to Fish & Game. "I need help here," I said. "There's an animal. Up in the Oakland Hills, on Alvarado Street. Someone's going to get hurt," I blurted out, realizing none of this made sense, talking to no one. By the time the message might be gotten, it would be much too late. So I put my phone away and kept following, keeping my distance. The animal, a couple of houses ahead of me now, had drifted back to the roadside, and then, after dropping its snout to the ground, flung its head back. And for a moment I thought maybe it had found what it was looking for, something to eat, and, satiated, would cross back over, disappear into the canyon. And then all would be fine. I could continue my walk uphill, circling around, and go home and tell someone my strange story. If only my husband were alive. But then the animal started gagging, spitting something out. A rock, maybe. Then it staggered to the middle of the road again and, craning its neck, looked back at me, this time as if it really saw me, and, arching its back, let out a terrible yowl and then swung its head back around. I heard a car horn and, looking past the animal, I spotted a shiny Jeep at the road's edge, where a young man, half out of the driver's seat, was waving his arms at me. Then, he waved his phone. "Can't get through to anyone," he shouted. "What should we do?"

"The police won't come out," I shouted. "There's a firehouse back up that way though." I pointed where I'd come from. "I'll see if they can help." I looked over at the animal now. It was moving down toward the Jeep. Then I heard an engine gunning, a car lower down speeding up, and the young man suddenly scrambled over to the side of the road and started picking up rocks and tossing them at the animal, the car now rounding the corner, then braking, screeching its tires, as the animal slowly wandered out of the way.

I continued back up, retracing my steps, hopeful, almost happy that I might find help, that someone else might care.

Since my husband had died, I'd cut myself off. Only recently were people starting to come out, get near each other, now that the pandemic was waning.

"What happened?" From above the gardener with the rake greeted me again.

"It's still down there, heading toward the Claremont Hotel. I'm going up to the firehouse to see if they can help."

"Oh, that's bad," the man said. "An animal like that."

I kept walking. After going around a bend, I was now on the other side. There I could hear the distant hum of the highway, cars now back on the roads. Two blocks later I was at the firehouse, a small, square windowless building with a flag pole in front and a patio and soda machine off to the side. It had been built after the firestorm, though no fire like that had ever burned here since. I rang the bell. When the door cracked opened, a barrel-chested man in a navy T-shirt stood behind it.

"There's a sick animal on the road," I said. "Could be rabid. I think it might bite someone."

He opened the door a little more. "An animal? What kind?"

"I'm not sure. I've never seen anything like it before," I said.

"You mean like a wild animal?"

Another man came up behind him, shorter, stouter, gray-haired and crossed his arms. "Ma'am, we fight fires. We're not equipped to deal with animals."

"But you work for the city. Can't you call someone?"

The man behind the door shook his head. "Who?"

"But the animal's suffering. It's sick."

The men looked at each. Then the older man, stepping closer, said, "Look, we really feel for you, but we wouldn't know what to do."

I started back downhill. I really hadn't walked that far, but I was feeling drained. If only the animal had veered into the canyon and disappeared. There, no doubt, it wouldn't last long. But even death by mountain lion seemed better than being run over, starving, or dying from disease. But then the lion might go rabid.

I passed the gardeners again. Both of them were down on the road now, the one with the shears in the driver's seat of their truck.

Then the other one got in, leaving his door open. "Sorry," he said. "Do you need a ride or something? We can take you down."

"No one will do anything."

He sighed. "What can any of us do?" Then he shut the door.

I pulled out my phone again. But who was I going to call? I started walking quickly downhill. When I got to the place where the Jeep had been, it was gone, everything quiet. I looked over toward the canyon. Dipping steeply down, it climbed up high on the other side to an area the fire hadn't touched. Then I turned back to the road and looked both ways. It was chillier now, the fog blowing in. Up here it could quickly consume everything, sinking down low. No side-walks up here, it would be dangerous for me to keep going, drivers having little visibility. I could just go back down, go home. It would be much quicker than going full circle. Still, I turned around, started walking uphill again, toward the firehouse. When I got there, the top half of the flagpole had disappeared, but I could hear it clanking, the wind stronger now. After walking another short block, I turned left, and started my descent, having to take a circuitous route, most roads up here dead-ends. Then some twenty minutes later, as I came around a bend, I suddenly saw a large oval eye, a black pupil, gazing back at me.

You Are Being Watched! We look out for each other!

I must have passed that sign a hundred times. It should have made me thankful, being looked out for, that I hadn't been one of the six million that had died gasping for breath.

Hospital beds opening up now, respirators readily available, more immunizations, better treatments were to come, the worst over. But now, coming full circle, it was already too late. The fog in low and thick here, I wasn't sure I could find the stone steps down to the parking lot. Even the hotel, its grand turrets and balconies, had disappeared, swallowed up. And though it wasn't night time, it had gotten darker. Peering into the grayness, I wondered what had become of the animal, if it had staggered back into the canyon, or was nearby, lurking in the fog, waiting to reappear.

Little People

It was only a matter of crossing Kegan Road, a six-lane drag bordered by snow banks, without getting side-swiped, and driving a few blocks. But Justine was taking it slow, not even out of her subdivision yet, her tires rolling over the packed snow as she passed the uniform one- and two-story ranches, the split-levels, this the kind of house her parents had splurged on when they'd moved here to the Midwest, to a suburb not far from Lake Michigan.

Justine brought the car to a stop. Another blizzard due in tonight, plenty of people were already on the road, no doubt her mother among them. Spotting an opening, Justine accelerated just enough to get across without fishtailing, a skill she'd learned in Driver's Ed last year, even though the teacher, his arm looped around her headrest, had made her nervous as she navigated the icy roads near her school.

Headed down Kegan now, Justine saw the railroad tracks ahead. In better weather she could have walked, though no one here ever did that, even in summer. Two years ago, driving into their new subdivision for the first time, they'd passed snowy yard after snowy yard, all devoid of footprints or even a snowman, and her little brother Gabe, face pressed to the window, had asked, "Where are all the people?"

After passing over the tracks, Justine turned right at the next light and drove alongside the familiar, two-story, windowless box, which might be mistaken for a bomb shelter if not for its marble facade, glass entry doors, and of course its name—the Deerhaven Mall. Not that shopping was her aim; actually it was a rather sore point after last weekend's fight, her mother wanting her to buy this blouse and Justine wanting to buy that one, until it boiled over, and her mother slapped her right in the middle of the crowded mall.

Avoiding the front lots, Justine drove up to no-man's land, the second-story back lot. Had her mother been with her, she would have insisted that she park close to the doors. But today Justine parked as far away as possible. Who cared how cold it was? The dry, frozen air that "stole your breath," as Gabe described it, and the weather in general, were the only things she liked about the Midwest, how the meteorologists stood in front of the state map speaking the language of cold, "lake-effect snow" and "windchill" and in spring the language of wind, "funnel clouds" and "twisters." If only one had touched down, sucking them up, whirling them away.

Justine turned off the engine and set the emergency brake. Then she zipped up her parka, pulled on her hat, and got out. She entered at the food court, a series of stalls. Normally packed, today the neatly arranged tables and chairs were now vacant. But all the stalls appeared open. Eyeing two clerks on the outskirts—a pimply-faced boy in a pink and brown-striped Baskin-Robbins shirt and a blonde girl in a gingham Lemon Tree apron—she guessed that both went to her school; but the school, double the size of her previous one, felt like another giant mall, the cavernous hallways either teeming with kids or eerily silent.

After passing through the court, Justine scanned the mall, the flat, fluorescent bleakness of it. Then she unzipped her parka, pulled off her ski cap, and stuffed it in her pocket. Running her fingers through her bangs, she pulled them down over her forehead and then started down the first stretch, passing The Unlimited, Hats Off, Gadget Geeks,

Candleroma, Tiddlywinks, Henkel's Hosiery, Shoe Heaven, Hobbycraft, not bothering to turn into any, barely glancing at their windows. Already bored, she then drifted over to the railing and rested her elbows on it. Peering down to the lower level, a duplicate of the upper level, she spotted a man wearing a pea-green parka looking back up at her. He looked disheveled, his hair all tangled, his glasses askew. Instinctively she stepped back, sucking in her breath, then forward again only to see him now slowly waving his arms over his head as if stranded. She had no idea who he was, and she had no friends unless you counted the dopey girls from next door who did little else than put on lash-clumping mascara and get high. And there was something off about the man. People here dressed up to go to the mall. (Other than going out to eat or shoveling snow, what else was there to do here in winter?) But then again with her short, cropped hair, in her jeans and her parka and her plain, unmade face, she barely passed herself.

She looked back toward the food court. She could just turn around, head home. But she didn't see why she should have to. After all, for a change, she actually had a reason for being here, something she promised to buy. Plus, her mother, likely home by now, was probably already pistol-whipping her father: "You let her go out *in* a storm? Really?" as she unpacked cans of beans, tuna, fruit cocktail, provisions that would save them from consuming each other's bodies should the storm strand them for months.

Justine started walking again. Not one person in sight, she could have done cartwheels down the corridor. Approaching the end of it, she rounded the corner, passing Lord & Taylor, and came around the other side. Then she went back to the railing and saw only empty benches framed by faux plants below.

Resuming her journey, she started absently glancing at store windows, some still filled with holiday cheer—wrapped gifts beneath Christmas trees, faux snow falling. If she kept going, she'd soon be back to the food court, having covered half of the top floor. Normally, though, she'd spend hours here, endlessly circling the mall. But then there were always people around. Not that she spoke to any unless she happened to run into some school kids, but they usually just passed her by.

Justine drifted back to the railing again. Just to make sure. And it only took a quick glimpse to see he was back, this time parka open, pants unzipped, hands cupped. Gasping, she pulled back. Though she'd never even had a boyfriend, she knew exactly what he was doing. She looked ahead toward the escalator, worried he might come up it. If she could just get past it… She turned to the store in front of her. The Merry-Go-Round. Racks and racks of children's clothes. She'd have to go deep in, toward the back, where the register was, to get any help. And probably there'd be a kid, maybe a girl from her school, working there, if she was lucky, maybe a manager.

Taking a deep breath, she started heading toward the escalator, quickly at first, hoping to get past it before he came up it, but then a little slower, trying to calm herself. Then she stopped. The little people. "For the dollhouse, Justy. Daddy's almost done," Gabe had said, hugging her legs, making her promise, before he'd let go. Tentatively, Justine angled back over to the railing, craning her neck forward, trying to see the lower half of the escalator without him seeing her. Peeping Toms, exhibitionists—she'd learned about these kinds of men in health class. "Rarely graduating to serious crimes, they usually run off, trying to escape detection," her teacher had said. Justine stepped away from the railing, the man nowhere in sight now. Still, she knew she should leave. But still she didn't want to disappoint Gabe, her little brother "an accident," her mother had confessed over pie at the Pie Factory.

Justine started backtracking. Walking quickly, she passed store after store, knowing all she had to do was turn into one, ask for help. But still she kept going. Back at Hobbycraft, she went up to the counter where the clerk, a short, old lady with thin dyed hair, stood.

"Little people, please," Justine said.

"Little people? What kind would those be, dear?"

"You know." Justine lifted her hand and with her thumb and index, showing the size. "For dollhouses."

"Oh," the woman said, coming out from behind the counter. She barely reached Justine's shoulder. "Dollhouse people. Right over there. Aisle 3."

Justine glanced out toward the mall, then went over to the aisle, where large boxes, kits with brightly-colored pictures of houses—Bancroft Barn, Plum Hill, Cecil Cottage—and all the Dollhouse, Inc. accessories—paint, wallpaper, hardwood planks, carpet, windows—were farther down, miniature furniture in plastic packages, some in sets, *Bathroom Set/4 with Flowers*, $32.00. As she scanned the display for little people, she couldn't help looking back down the aisle though, out toward the mall, and then, refocusing, she spotted a family-set hanging from a hook. The only one left, she grabbed it and went back to the counter.

"Find what you need, dear?" The woman slipped on a pair of glasses.

As she wrote out a sales check in large, slow cursive, and then rang up the sale, Justine asked, "Did you see a man here in a green parka?"

The woman looked up. "Why, no, I haven't seen anyone. Didn't you hear, dear? Storm's already in. Mall's closing early. Why?"

I think someone's following me. Please help me, she wanted to say. But then she'd have to tell what he was doing. And she knew what would happen. Her mother would blame her father for letting her go, and then her mother, thinking the whole story made up, would blame her. There'd be a fight. Gabe would have to cover his ears. Worse, her mother would blab it all over the place, making it more than it was. And the police would never find the man.

"There you go." The clerk handed her change and a small brown bag.

Back into the mall, Justine took a tentative step toward the railing then turned away, afraid of what she'd see. Clutching the bag of little people, she sped up, passing all the stores, rounding the Lord & Taylor corner, fast approaching the escalator again. But then someone was coming up it, and she veered away, hugging the stores, all of them dark, closed now. But it was too late. The man was already angling toward her, trying to cut her off, and she thought if only she could scream. But who would hear her? And now his hands were on her, pulling her toward him, and hers, to her surprise, were shoving him away. Then, suddenly free, she was running through the food court, out the back doors, into the blinding whiteness of falling snow.

In her car, she locked the doors. Engine started, she switched on the wipers, trying to clear the windshield. Before shifting into reverse, she looked out her own window, half expecting his face to be there, pressed in, smashed up. After backing out and then shifting into drive, she tried to get some traction, the back wheels spinning. Then, suddenly, the car started moving forward. Out of the lot now, and on the road out, she kept checking the rearview mirror. Stay calm. Go slow. If you lose control, tap the brake If that fails, pump the emergency brake. But she couldn't help it—pushing down hard on the accelerator now, she was speeding, the back of the car fishtailing, and still in her rearview mirror nothing but white. Ahead though she thought she could make out a blurry green circle, and she sped toward it. Then as she started to make the wide left onto Kegan, headlights suddenly flashed through her back window, and she pressed even harder, sending herself into the intersection, into a spin. And when it was all over, somehow she ended up pointed in the right direction—or at least she thought so.

Later, back home at dinner, it was all Justine could to keep herself from constantly getting up, checking the living room window.

Her mother, frowning, put her fork down. "Why so antsy?"

Gabe peered over his hot dog at her. "Did you get the little people, Justy?"

She'd almost forgotten—running out of the mall, she must have dropped them. "Oh, sorry, Gabe, they were all out."

"Out?" Her mother raised her eyebrows. "Really?"

"The clerk said they're on order." Justine averted her eyes.

"Well, isn't that interesting. Who'd think they'd be so popular?" Her mother eyed her father. "A shortage of little people—do you believe that?"

Fork in the air, her father shot her mother a sideways look. "Why not?"

Her mother turned back to her. "Well, I hope you cleaned up the patio at least. Like I told you."

After dinner, in her bedroom, Justine closed her door and turned off her lights. Over at the window she watched the snow, lighter now, floating down from the night sky. Clearly the weatherman had gotten it wrong. Then she heard her doorknob jiggle and felt a whoosh. The light went on.

"Why are you in the dark?" Her mother walked over to the window and stood beside her. She put her hands on her hips. "What are you looking at?"

Justine peered at the street lamp, the curve of its neck, the halo of light. She didn't see why they had to move here, why they couldn't just pack up, go home.

Her mother straightened up. "Do you speak?"

"I don't know. The boogeyman, I guess." Justine couldn't help herself. Nobody could—her father always down in the basement hammering away, Gabe always clinging to her, her mother always shopping for disaster. She thought of that family she'd bought in the mall, encased snugly in plastic, lost somewhere.

"By the way I don't believe that for a minute. About the little people. Gabe was crestfallen. Did you see him?" Her mother sat back on the foot of the bed and let out a long sigh. "Well, the school wants to leave him behind again. They think he's depressed. What am I supposed to do?"

JUSTINE LOOKED over at the amber glow of her clock—3:00 am—and slipped out of bed, the sound that woke her coming from inside the house. Through the hallway and down the stairs she went. Then, in the dining room, she dropped down a few more steps into the playroom, where the basement door was, a dim light beneath it.

After opening the door, she went halfway down and sat on a step. Her father, his back to her now, was hammering as usual, and for a moment she thought he might stop, turn around, see her this time. No doubt other people, sensing a presence, would. But she knew her father wasn't like other people. He was consumed by things—his tools, his workbench, nuts and bolts, the little screws in their little drawers, her favorite red vice. Sometimes when no one was home, she liked to put her fingers between its jaws and turn the lever. She looked at her fingers now and then at her father. Hammer down now, he was bent over, doing the delicate work, shingling, gluing on tiny shakes, these houses backless so you could see inside, into the rooms where the little people lived.

Justine went back upstairs. In the playroom she went over to the sliding glass door and turned on the patio light. *Like I told you.* Her mother's dinner-table voice—haughty and hateful—came back to her as she peered at the dark feathers of the small birds, four this time, she was expected to clean up. Confused, they sometimes flew into the glass and dropped to the ground and froze.

Back to Eve

She'd been built for better things. Surely the mannequins, sentenced to eternal duty at the scalloped rim of the department, would think the very same thing if they were only human. If they were only human, they would unscrew themselves from their pedestals and beat it to the escalator in their Jonquil peignoirs, Natori slippers, scant Lejaby bras and panties. And if Tess had the courage she'd come out from behind the counter and follow suit, taking the escalator down to freedom; maybe others from the lower floors would join in too, creating a snake-like chain of women and mannequins all walking off the job, out the front doors, into the teeming traffic of San Francisco's Union Square. Such was the fantasy that propelled Tess through another tedious workday of panties and girdles and bra fittings. It wasn't so much the merchandise—any sales associate worth her commission knew merchandise was merchandise. Nor was it so much the naked bodies—in high school locker rooms she'd seen plenty, but those were all young, undamaged bodies on the brink of flowering, whereas most of what wound up naked in a Saks Fifth Avenue dressing room had slipped over the brink into the no-man's land of cellulite and sagging breast. Cornered in a small, mirrored dressing room with such creatures, Tess, only twenty-one, had wondered if she'd graduated college only to girdle and wire *the mature woman,* as Saks called her, back to Eve. Worse yet, just three months into her job, she feared she might get fired. *Tess lacks the proper enthusiasm for lingerie* is what her manager Eleanor, a giraffe-like woman with owlish eyes, wrote on her three-month review. Downstairs, in the bowels of HR, she'd been berated for her ignorance, her lack of enthusiasm for what made women tick—underwear!

On her lunch break now, Tess crossed the street, stepping into Union Square, its small, scrubby park boxed in by other department stores, the only greenery the hedges. With all the pigeons flapping about, pecking at the ground, and the incessant din of traffic, it was hardly a sanctuary; still, it beat the employee cafeteria, a drab basement room with vending machines and lockers.

Tess sat down on a bench and peered inside her bag at today's rations—tuna fish and an apple. Her fear of losing her job and knowing she'd eventually have to move out of her boyfriend's apartment had put her in a bind. He'd been nice enough though after dumping her, after saying he didn't love her, letting her sleep downstairs on the couch until she could save first and last month's rent. And worse yet, despite his rejection of her or because of it, she was all the more love-sick for him, wondering where he was now, this his day off, if he was upstairs at his desk, the sun streaming through the window, writing a poem. A poetry class was where they'd first met last year, in senior seminar, in the Cathedral of Learning, a giant white tower, a stately thing, some forty-two floors up, piercing the University of Pittsburgh sky.

She pulled out her sandwich and took a bite, the bread slightly stale, the tuna heavy on mayo, while she peered at the pigeons vying for crumbs and the carefree shoppers gliding by, passing spare-changers holding their cups out. Then someone sat down beside her. She didn't see why, an empty bench right beside hers. But then again this was California where everyone's your friend.

"That bad?" the man asked. He leaned back against the bench and slid his hands in his pant pockets. He was dressed in a pin-striped suit, his face pocked, eyes lizard-like. Way older than her.

Tess scooted away a little. A fly started buzzing around her head and then landed on her sandwich.

"They vomit when they do that, you know," the man said.

Tess had heard that before but didn't know if it was true. She slipped her sandwich back in her bag just in case and pulled out her apple. Biting into it, she gnashed it around in her mouth, hoping the man would just leave.

"Secretary or salesgirl?" He tried again.

Tess swallowed what she was chewing and took another bite, keeping her gaze on the pigeons, two of them now squabbling over something she couldn't see.

"Either way," the man said, "they can't pay you much."

"Either way I don't see why it matters to you." Tess winced a little; she hadn't meant to be so smart. But getting rid of a man wasn't so easy, getting rid of one in California even harder. Of course it was really *she* that was being gotten rid of. If only her boyfriend had fessed up *before* she'd boarded the plane, flying cross country to be with him.

"It must be difficult, the kind of work you do," the man said.

"The kind of work I do." She repeated back his words, even though she knew it was childish. Crossing her legs, she took another bite of her apple. Then, studying the apple, she rotated it a little, the inside already starting to brown.

"Okay. The kind of work you *want* to do."

As it turned out the kind of work she wanted to do—marketing or publishing—she couldn't unless she was willing to type, file, greet: *so and so agency. How can I direct your call?* Tess lowered her apple and turned to him. She'd seen her fair share of these men her father's age on their lunch breaks, in their suits, prowling the department, deep in the trees, feeling up the bras, fingering the peignoirs. And she'd almost felt sorry for them, furtive as they were, shopping for their mistresses, while her co-workers, the ancient gargoyles of *Nightwear*—Miss Zena and Miss Miriam—readied themselves to pounce. *Her cup size? The shape of her breasts? Waist? Hips? And her bottom, sir? Like this or like that?* They'd used their gnarled hands, rattling off questions, these well-off widows only working out of boredom, until the men, embarrassed, looking for escape, dropped a bundle.

"So what is it you want?" Tess finally asked the man, thinking it better to get the upper hand Miss Zena or Miss Miriam style. Thirty minutes of her break left, she wasn't moving.

"Want?"

Tess dropped her half-eaten apple into her bag. "I have a boyfriend." She hated resorting to that. Worse, it wasn't even true anymore, though she couldn't help thinking of her boyfriend slipping in bed late nights smelling of garlic and oil after his shift at Yokomonos where he cooked at tables, juggling knives, sending shrimp soaring to the empty plates of amazed patrons, how when they had sex, he would turn off all the lights. Never show his body.

"Well, you don't need be so rude about it," the man said, getting up. He pulled a card out of his pocket and dropped it on the bench. "In case you need me."

BACK ON THE FLOOR NOW, Tess assumed her position behind the lingerie counter. As she often did, she gazed beyond the bra trees to the mannequins, the twin sentinels at the department's edge, hands on their hips, elbows jutting out, pelvis thrust slightly forward. There was always something pouty about their perfect faces, these tall, leggy women with page-boy wigs and small breasts dressed in silk peignoirs. But who could blame them, their faces based on real women, she'd read. Tess looked down at the lingerie counter, inside, a pink Galina bra, a Russian import, with matching silk panties, sachet pouch, and garter. Then, down the length of the counter, she spotted the afternoon's penance—her manager must have dumped the stack there while she'd been at lunch. Ladyette taffeta slips. Style 1260. Bone. All mediums and larges. Plain Jane. Popular with the old maids.

"Good afternoon, Miss Tess!" Bra-fitter extraordinaire Miss Florida, in for the late shift, was now winding her way around the trees. All in white today, she looked nurse-like, except for her dark pony tail tied neatly with a bright red ribbon, and the clear plastic purse all Saks associates were required to carry to make sure they weren't stealing.

"Afternoon, Miss Florida," Tess said, as Miss Florida went into the stockroom and then, before coming out, slipped down the hallway to the dressing rooms, hauling out a heap of bras. "Awful lot of traffic this morning, I see." She dropped the heap on the counter.

"A flurry right before lunch," Tess said, avoiding Miss Florida's eyes.

"That so?" Miss Florida sighed.

Tess nodded, though it had in fact been dead all morning. During these times, in the windowless silence of the store, when she was alone, it was hard not to slip into a reverie, to become morose, bitter. And so this morning when she came in she hadn't bothered to do a sweep of the dressing rooms, to clean out last night's mess.

Miss Florida's expert fingers started untangling the bras while Tess, feeling guilty, worked hard on the slips, tearing off plastic, then pulling out the cheap plastic hangers, replacing them with sturdier ones all the while trying to find that *raison d'etre* for product: *Fabulous! Just what we need—slips! Adjustable straps, ¾ length, scalloped neck.* But, holding a slip up against her own body for Miss Florida to see, all Tess managed was a "Look at these."

"Mmhm," Miss Florida said, not even bothering to lift her head as she began sliding bras onto small plastic hangers.

Tess remembered her mother dragging her into a department like this when she was twelve, even though she was essentially flat chested. Her mother always rushing things. Womanhood and all. But first chance Tess got she chucked those baby-pink stretch jobs and hadn't worn a bra since. So maybe her manager was right, that in the broader world of bra-wearing women, she lacked the proper enthusiasm, was an utter failure, flunking out at womanhood. Still, she'd made her sales quotas, likely the only reason she hadn't been fired on the spot.

Tess looked over at Miss Florida now. Out in the trees, she was hanging bras. "Really," Tess said, trying again, "if I were to ever wear a slip, I might wear this one."

"Look, child," Miss Florida said, pausing in front of the Paulina Plus tree, where all the heavily padded bras hung awkwardly, each bra bumping into the one in front of it, "you'll need to do better than that if you're going to save yourself."

She knew Miss Florida knew she was in trouble, *an educated girl in a dead-end job like this*, what Miss Florida had muttered the first time she saw her.

Miss Florida marched back around the counter and gazed out into the trees, at some distant horizon. "Lord, I'll never understand why rich people are such slobs? You'd think God made them that way, and we their maids." Her lips sealed, she puffed out her cheeks, holding her breath, and stared at Tess as if she were one of the female slobs for whom her job had been created and then, letting the air out, started laughing.

Smiling, Tess came out from behind the counter with all the slips draped over her arm as if she were a waiter, hanging them by size.

"Remember that one in the red suit last weekend?" Miss Florida asked. "Took in a dozen Diors. Now what do you think she was doing when I knocked on her door?"

Tess glanced back at Miss Florida. "What—stealing?" Tags ripped off new bras were always turning up on dressing room floors, and old bras in the garbage pails. The most expensive ones had sensors though. Women wearing long billowy skirts had to stuff those between their legs to avoid setting off the alarms.

Miss Florida shook her head. "Worse."

Worse? Only last week Tess had to call security on two topless women snapping pictures of each other in G-strings and the week before that a couple having chair sex. How could Miss Florida top that?

"The woman," Miss Florida said, stepping back behind the counter and putting her hands on her hips, "was using the dressing room as a bathroom. That's right. I got a good look at her, through the door slats. Security built them that way to keep people from stealing, but this one, she wasn't stealing. She was squatting with the garbage pail up over her bottom." Miss Florida shook her head. "You'd think she couldn't get to the restroom. Only a few steps away. All those fancy clothes. Mmhm." She rubbed her hands together and nodded as if what she'd witnessed had confirmed some long-held suspicion. "I'm going to wash my hands."

When Tess got home that night, the apartment was quiet. She went upstairs to the bedroom, though she hadn't slept there since he'd dumped her, and over to her boyfriend's desk, on it a pad and some pens, a small spider plant in the remaining light. Back in Pittsburgh, the poem he'd read aloud in senior seminar, the one that got her, about San Francisco, the Tenderloin, where prostitutes gathered at corner bodegas as the night time fog swept in, had fascinated her. And when she'd first moved in, before it all went bad, he'd shown her his drafts. But today, the pad blank, Tess turned to head back downstairs, but something caught her eye, lying crumpled on the shag carpet near the bed, a pair of panties. Bikini. Striped. Cotton. Size 5. She'd worked lingerie long enough that she could tell size without checking the tag.

Tess grabbed a pen from her boyfriend's desk and, kneeling, slipped it in one of the leg openings, lifting it up. That's how Miss Florida handled these things—moldy bras clients had worn for years and decided to return. Dangling the bra in the air, Miss Florida, incredulous, eyes bulging. "You want to return this?" But the specimen now dangling before Tess was immaculate—colors unfaded, no evidence of wear and tear. Fruit of the Loom. She could see the label now. Way below Saks standard.

THE NEXT DAY Tess was back at work. If her boyfriend had come in last night, she hadn't heard him, not from the downstairs where she slept, nor did she bother peeking into his bedroom again when she'd gone upstairs to shower. For all she knew he could have been in there with her replacement, the size 5 Fruit of the Loom. But Tess didn't have time to fret, the department having a presentation first thing. And now more than ever she needed to keep her job.

At work now, Tess joined Miss Florida and Eleanor, who were already behind the counter while the rep, on the other side, was unpacking her wares.

"Tess," Eleanor said, "Can you please go over and fetch Miss Zena and Miss Miriam? I think they should be here too."

As Tess crossed over into *Nightwear* she could hear their register beeping, Saks' recent transition from handwritten sales checks to computerized registers having thrown lots of the older associates into a tailspin.

"Damn machine," Miss Zena said, as she stood beside Miss Miriam whose quivering hand hung above the register, her finger tapping a random key every so often.

Tess came around and punched in the opening code.

"Oh, thank god," Miss Zena said. "I thought I was going to go deaf."

"Eleanor wants you over in lingerie for a presentation," Tess said.

"What for?" Miss Zena asked. "If it's about underwear, we don't want to go."

"Yeah," Miss Miriam said, "we sell nightgowns."

"Well she wants you over there anyway," Tess said, as she turned to make her way back, the two trailing behind her.

"Ladies," Eleanor said, now that they were all assembled, "this is Miss Lithgow. She's going to introduce us to a new product we'll be carrying. *The Woman Within*. Prosthetic breasts for cancer victims."

"Oh, Jesus," Miss Zena muttered under her breath. "I'm not going near those." In her black dress today, her white hair swirled on her head, she might have been a beauty if not for her beady eyes and sizable beak. Still, she was better preserved than Miss Miriam who wore her hair in a girlish gray bouffant, her face mummified, imploding.

"Well, it's about time," said Miss Florida, who knew something about cancer, having lost two husbands, one a boxer, the other an alcoholic, to it. When the floor was quiet Miss Florida would tell Tess about them.

"It's about giving back to women what was taken from them," the rep said smiling pleasantly as she lifted the lid off a small floral box. "It's about making women whole." She let that sentence hang in the air as she peered at each of them, sizing up the mission. Then, she reached into the box and parted the tissue, saying, "This, ladies, is a breast." On her palm rested a large, dollop-shaped breast. "Feel it." The rep handed the breast to Tess, who held it in her palms uncomfortably like a dead animal. Not at all like a human breast, it seemed to her much heavier and oddly cold and shiny, a poor forgery. Just as Tess was getting ready to hand it off to Miss Florida, the rep scooped it back up again. "Surely, ladies, no breast can be complete without a nipple." She snapped open a tiny compact and lifted out a small, flesh-colored suction cup.

Miss Miriam's hand rose tentatively, her lower lip quivering now. "How much do those cost?"

"Breast and nipple together run $400.00."

"Good god!" Miss Zena gasped as she pressed her hand to her chest, pretending to keel over as the rep said, "The cost is actually modest compared to reconstruction—those breasts usually wind up hard as rocks and positioned all wrong."

"Let me see that breast," Miss Florida said, taking it from the rep. Poking and prodding at it, she turned the breast this way and that way, then shook her head. "What the Lord won't do. How's a poor woman without insurance supposed to afford such a thing?"

The rep, frowning, took the breast back and laid it in its bed of tissue. "You never want to lay a breast in a woman's hand. She'll think it too heavy. You'll want to slip the breast in the Celeste Nest bra first." She held up a cotton bra by its straps, a giant white bat with its wings spread. Into a pocket sewn within the cup she slipped the breast.

Tess peered away from the thing. She didn't know which was worse—getting stuck in a dressing room with a woman round-shouldered by quadruple D breasts and having to literally bend a Betsy Busty around her or a woman halved without a breast. Though she'd only seen one mastectomy, when she was sixteen and working after-school at Lord & Taylor and got pulled from Children's to cover over in Lingerie, the sight of it was still vivid—where the breast should have been was a zipper, as if the breast had been snatched and the skin hastily zipped closed.

WHEN TESS GOT HOME that night, she was exhausted. She didn't know how much longer she could stand the job—the large-breasted who wanted smashing down, the small-breasted who needed plumping up, the saggy-breasted that needed lifting, and now the halved women wanting to be whole—all punctuated by long periods of silence, of tedium. The only customers she liked were the transvestites who rang her up always knowing what they wanted—Maidenwear style 1725, a front-snapping, sheer-cup, underwire bra—and usually they ordered in bulk. In the kitchen now she sat at the very table where her boyfriend had dumped her, saying, "I don't think I can love you, but you can stay if you want." Though hurt, she hadn't fussed, hadn't cried, yelled, pleaded. She'd simply cleared away the dishes and then slept on the couch. For weeks after she and her boyfriend only bumped into each other in the kitchen or in the bathroom like estranged roommates. Some nights he didn't come home at all. And then the Fruit of the Loom underwear...

Tess reached into her coat pocket, emptying everything— keys, bus pass, pennies, old receipts—on the table, and there it was, that card from that hideous man in the park. *Eve Unhinged*, a crude sketch of a topless woman on it, her breasts pendulous, lips parted. A phone number.

The door opened and in stepped her boyfriend. "Hey," he said, shutting the door and then stepping into the living room.

Tess, feeling her face warm, blush a little, turned away. She'd no business snooping around his room, and it was nice of him to let her stay, to save up her money. But the Fruit of the Loom...she was trying not to let it bother her.

"Haven't seen you for a while. You okay?" He dropped his backpack alongside the couch. She couldn't help tracking him with her eyes, thinking, as he headed toward the kitchen, passing her, that he might stop, come up behind her, resting his hands on her shoulders like he used to before slipping them down her blouse.

Acknowledgments

Gratefully acknowledged are the following publications, where stories in this collection first appeared:

"The Hike" (*Santa Clara Review*)
"Ursa Major" (*The Bear Essential*)
"Rock, River, Salmon, Sky" (*Black Zinnias*)
"Every Small Thing" (*Full Circle: A Journal of Art & Literature*)
"Desert Draw" (*Deep Wild*)
"The Prank" (*Rosebud*)
"The Keeper" (*Oyster River Pages*)
"Goldfish & Women" (*Penumbra*)
"Nell" (*Wilderness House Literary Review*)
"Safe" & "A Proper Ballerina" (*The Chamber*)
"Like Human" (*Santa Fe Quarterly*)
"Little People" (*Flying Island Literary Journal*)
"A Pretty Picture" (*JONAH* magazine)
"Hurt" (*South Dakota Review*)
"The Fugitive Widow" (*The Coe Review*)
"Back to Eve" (*Otherwise Engaged Literature & Arts Journal*)

Many thanks to Dr. Ross K. Tangedal, Brett Hill, Sam Bjork, Sophie McPherson, and the rest of the Cornerstone Press for shepherding *Like Human* into the world.

Janet Goldberg is the author of *The Proprietor's Song* (2023). Her short stories and poems have appeared in a wide-range of journals, including *Oyster River Pages, Zone 3, Snake River Nation, The Dallas Review,* and *Poetry East.* She serves as the fiction editor for *Deep Wild* and teaches writing in California's Bay Area.